The IHOP Papers

The IHOP Papers

Ali Liebegott

CARROLL & GRAF PUBLISHERS
NEW YORK

THE IHOP PAPERS

Carroll & Graf Publishers
An Imprint of Avalon Publishing Group, Inc.
245 West 17th Street, 11th Floor
New York, NY 10011

AVALON
publishing group incorporated

First Carroll & Graf edition 2007

This is a work of fiction and is in no way authorized or endorsed by IHOP Corp.

Library of Congress Cataloging-in-Publication Data is available.

ISBN-13: 978-0-78671-794-1
ISBN-10: 0-7867-1794-7

Interior design by Ivelisse Robles Marrero

Printed in the United States of America
Distributed by Publishers Group West

For my parents
&
for the queer waiters & waitresses of the world

"The purpose of life is to be defeated by greater and greater things."

—Rainer Maria Rilke

1

FIRST OF ALL, I'm twenty and I've never slept with anyone. I've been in AA for three years. That's how I ended up in San Francisco. I moved here from Southern California to seduce my philosophy teacher from community college, Irene. Whenever I imagine having sex with a woman, I picture myself drinking goblets of wine in dimly lit rooms and touching her clavicles as if they were the original pages of the Bible, so old and sacred, thin and transparent. Was the Bible written on stone or scrolls? Regardless, you know what I mean; lightly, as if her clavicles were the thin, almost transparent pages of a very old Bible, and I was the archaeologist who'd fallen into this glorious excavation.

You have to have some balls to title your book the Bible. That's not what I'm titling my book. My book is called *The IHOP Papers*, because it's about working at the International House of Pancakes— home of the blue, pointy roof, and the ugliest waitress dress in existence. Oh god, if you've never seen the uniform, you should. It's enough to make you want to kill yourself, if you didn't already want to. It's navy blue with poofy sleeves and a country floral apron. The rust-colored flowers in the apron match the booths in the smoking section, and the material is a bulletproof polyester blend.

I am not a star waitress by any means. I'd like to be, though. I want to be the kind of waitress who can carry five plates on each arm and glide around the room doing a dance of pancakes.

When I called my mom to tell her I got a job working nights she said, "Francesca, I worry about you coming home so late on the bus."

"Please," I said, "my uniform is so thick, even if someone stabbed me I wouldn't get hurt."

We also have to wear nude stockings and white nurse shoes.

*　*　*

Lots of people hate gay people.

You can tell who they are because they start sentences with, "It's not like I hate gay people."

When I took a speech class at community college, I did my persuasive speech on gay rights. I took the side that it's wrong to murder gay people. When I went to the library to do research, I was petrified someone would think I was gay, so I tried to seem nonchalant when I asked the librarian where the gay books were.

"Excuse me!" I shouted. "I'm doing a report on gay rights, do you have any books?" It was a reverse psychology of sorts. If I seemed confident about my book request, she wouldn't suspect I was gay. The blood vessels in my cheeks and earlobes throbbed as I waited desperately for her reply.

She pointed me toward the gay books, probably thinking, "Another little dyke hiding behind a class report." I grabbed the first one I saw off the shelf and ran to the checkout desk.

My speech ended up sucking, because I had unknowingly grabbed a gossip almanac of gay people through history.

"You should be careful who you make fun of because lots of people are gay, especially famous people like Michael Jackson, Anne Frank, Martina Navratilova, and Janis Joplin."

Everyone clapped. My speech had a dynamic conclusion like the teacher had suggested on day one.

"Leave them with something to think about," Ms. Brink had said.

I was walking back to my seat surrounded by applause when Ms. Brink pulled on my arm and said, "Can you stay after class for a minute?"

"Sure," I said, glowing with pride. She's probably going to ask me to join the debate team.

After the last student gave a speech on the importance of fiber optics in today's society, everyone filtered out of the room.

"Francesca," Ms. Brink began, as she walked toward me in her abusively floral pantsuit, "what sources did you use for your speech?"

"The library only had one good book, called *Top Secret Gay Stars*," I said.

Ms. Brink then proceeded to lecture me on the difference between reliable and unreliable resources. She said I didn't know for sure if these famous people in history were gay, *especially Anne Frank*.

"I'm going to have to give you a C, since part of the assignment is to do responsible research," she said.

"Okay," I said, feeling less disappointed by the C than by the prospect that Janis Joplin might not be gay.

Before I moved to San Francisco, right after I graduated from high school, I drove around in a flower truck delivering flowers all day and pretending all sorts of things. For instance, I fantasized that on my daily route I'd end up meeting famous people. My favorite fantasy was that I'd ring a doorbell, holding a tall bouquet that covered my face, and when the door opened, Hope from *Days of Our Lives* would be standing there. Seeing the flowers, she'd gasp with delight and reach to take them from me. That's when she'd see my busted lip and black eye.

"Oh my god, your poor face. Come in, come in," she'd say, "let me put something on those cuts."

"Don't worry 'bout me, ma'am. I just need you to sign right here on the X," I'd spit out raspily, pushing my clipboard forward while flicking my tongue toward the blood in the corner of my mouth. Insisting, in a half-mother-half-whore manner, Hope would drag me in for a glass of water, stare into my eyes, and dab iodine on all my cuts. Then I'd bow my head into her chest, tracing the tip of my nose across her collarbones in a way that she'd always wanted her husband Bo to do but he never did.

I'm real big on collarbones. I love how the curved bones push up delicately against the skin. One hard punch and you could smash them. There should be a Collarbone Museum, where the most spectacular collarbones in the world are behind red velvet rope. If I ever took Hope from *Days of Our Lives* to the Collarbone Museum, I'd point to all the beautiful ivory-shaped bones that looked like whittled willow branches and say, "That dogshit can't compare to your collarbones."

Eventually, Hope and I would live in a one-bedroom apartment together with Christmas tree lights strung up in the kitchen. After I made love to her, I'd go to the kitchen and drink milk right from the carton, shutting the refrigerator door with a small click, before walking back to our bed, my bare feet sticking to the dirty linoleum with each step.

I've always wanted Christmas lights strung up in my kitchen, but I've never done it. The kitchen I have now is small—there's a sink, a stove, a refrigerator, a wall, and my table where I'm typing this. It's an old apartment but I love it. The window in the kitchen opens up onto a fire escape. Sometimes I sit out there. Once my AA sponsor Maria and I ate strawberries on the fire escape, and I told her all my little problems, never mentioning the big problem, which is that I'm attracted to her. Maria had gotten new combat boots the day we sat on the fire escape and she was putting pink laces in them as I ate strawberries and watched the sunlight make slat-shaped shadows on the ground beneath us. When she was done lacing her boots, I reached out and petted the round leather toes. Desire moved from my hand and up through my body as I stroked the black leather.

"Like puppies," I said.

She laughed, glancing nervously at my hand.

Maria is the most beautiful woman I've ever met. She has jet-black hair and the sides are growing in from a mohawk. Her eyes are this deep green and she always wears glossy red lipstick. I wish we could hang out for longer periods of time, but she always has some-place to go. Technically an AA sponsor is supposed to help the sponsee stay sober by sharing their own experience, strength, and hope. But I always pick my sponsors by who is the most beautiful woman in the room.

In case you're keeping score, so far I love three people:

Irene, my community college philosophy teacher

Hope from *Days of Our Lives*

Maria, my AA sponsor

(I'm not counting Janis Joplin because she's dead.)

2

WHEN I GOT hired at IHOP I still lived with Irene because it was right after I moved to San Francisco. Irene moved here to be with two other former students who are now her lovers. They live in Simplicity House. I didn't want to live there with Jenny and Gustavo. If it was just Irene and me it would be different, but I can't stand to see her in love with Gustavo when I'm so in love with her. I just stayed there long enough to save some money and get my own place.

On my second day in San Francisco I went looking for a job in my interview outfit: black jeans, a black sweater, and my eight-dollar black Thrifty drugstore shoes. My mom named them "postman shoes" when I first showed them to her. They were the most presentable shoes I owned for job searching, even though they had a paper plate for a sole and no arch support. Before I left the house Jenny told me there were a bunch of restaurants in the Marina where tourists ate, including an IHOP filled with freaks. I think there is an indisputable link between freaks and a bottomless coffee cup.

"You should totally work at IHOP!" Gustavo said. "This lady goes there every Sunday and lets her poodle sleep in her purse while she eats her pancakes. Wouldn't it be cool to work at a place with freaks like that?"

Maybe I could write about all the freaks, but IHOP wasn't my first choice as a place to work. First I wanted to go to North Beach, where Jenny said all the Italian bakeries were. I left Simplicity House at 8 A.M. and walked from Pacific Heights to North Beach, inquiring in every restaurant, bakery, café, and ice-cream shop on the way. It was stupid to have started so early in the morning, since most places weren't even open. Each time I walked in somewhere the same thing happened: the cashier leaned over the counter to take my order.

"I was actually wondering if you were hiring," I'd say.

"Oh," the disappointed cashier would say.

Sometimes he or she would go ask a manager, but most places didn't even have me fill out an application. At first I felt guilty not buying anything even though I wanted to eat all the Italian pastries and cookies, but I promised myself I wouldn't spend any money until I got a job. And I wanted to get a job before lunch.

By one o'clock, I had a headache from smoking too much and my hunger had grown into some sort of electric prodder that prompted me to jaywalk defiantly in front of delivery trucks. The postman shoes had rubbed two nice-sized blisters on each of my pinky toes, and even though I hadn't wanted to spend the dollar on bus fare I wandered over to a bus shelter and found Lombard Street on the map. I needed the 45 to get to IHOP, so I lit a cigarette and waited.

When the bus came I fed my dollar into the slot and slid into a seat next to the window. It felt so good to sit down. Out the window, the sky was an amazing 1960s Ford Falcon, powder blue. Watching the ornately designed apartment buildings go by out the window rejuvenated me a bit. I couldn't believe I was actually in San Francisco. *I live here. I live where Irene lives.* I dangled my fingers out the open bus window to touch the place where I now lived.

Soon the blue roof of IHOP appeared among some other buildings on the street, so I pulled the white cord to stop the bus. Even though the sun was shining, it was cold in the Marina. The breeze whipped icily into my face as I walked toward the slanted blue roof. The restaurant was relatively empty and filled with a muted mix of cigarette smoke and sunlight that had slipped in through the barely opened rust-colored mini blinds. A short man came out to greet me.

"Table for one?" he asked cheerfully.

"I was actually wondering if you're hiring."

"Oh, sure," he said excitedly, "let me get you an application."

He minced his way behind the cash register to a shelf that had three large white binders on them, all labeled APPLICATION FLOW LOG. Inside the pocket in the binder he ripped an application off a pad for me. He seems gay, I thought hopefully.

"If you want you can fill it out now and then I can give it to the manager."

"Sure," I said. This felt like real progress after a day of getting the cold shoulder. Why hadn't I come to IHOP first?

"If you need anything, my name is Enrique," he said before prancing around to a counter of empty sugar bowls.

The air conditioner was cranked up so high my fingers felt numb. I filled out the application quickly, enraged at the tedium of writing down the same information for the twentieth time today. Did anyone ever really look at the application? It seemed like they just checked to see if the felony conviction box was marked. In front of me a dessert carousel spun. I stared sadly at a peach pie, realizing that all I'd consumed today was about thirteen cigarettes and a cup of coffee.

I don't know how long I spaced out watching the peach pie turn in circles, but Enrique startled me when I realized he was standing before me.

"I can bring your application to Julio now," he said.

I looked down at the application and saw I'd unconsciously written *help, help, help* all over the margins. *Fuck.* I doodle obsessively all the time. Reluctantly I handed Enrique the application. *Maybe no one will notice.*

About fifteen seconds later a tall, nervous man came around the corner with my application in his hand.

"I'm Julio, the manager."

"Hi," I said, standing up and shaking his hand.

"Can you start today at four?"

Two hours wasn't much time to walk back home, get changed, put my hair up into the regulation IHOP bun (no wisps, braids, or any hair hanging below the earlobes), buy nurse shoes, and get back to IHOP.

I was dying to show off my new uniform for a laugh but no one was home. Wearing the IHOP uniform is like wearing a freaky Halloween costume except it's not Halloween and no one thinks it's witty. Yet there was a part of wearing it those first days that felt like a badge of honor. I was a real worker, even though I'd had jobs since I was fifteen. Now I rode the bus in my waitress uniform.

Julio said Payless had the best deal on nurse shoes. So I went there and was shocked to see an entire aisle devoted to the white vinyl things. I found a pair that fit me and wore them out of the store, feeling, for a second, proud and grown up, like a waitress on a television show who had kids at home and an unemployed boyfriend. While I worked, he sat at my kitchen table and chain-smoked, waiting for our extensive relationship problems to disappear. In the backyard my children played with matches. . . .

I waited for the bus in my new getup. When the orange and white electric-powered bus creaked to a stop in front of me, I climbed the steps and dropped my quarters in the slot.

The bus driver looked me up and down and said, "Are you German?"

"I'm half German."

He stared at me for a second, and then pulled the bus away from the curb. How did he know I was German? He must think he knows me from somewhere. Whenever someone thinks they know me, it ends up being from AA. My brother Rich calls me a freak magnet when I tell him stories about people I've met. He's right. I do meet a lot of weird people. It's because I'm always sitting in bus stops on rainy nights with my arms all slit up. I'll explain that later, but normal people don't stop to chat in those situations. Between attracting freaks and being too lonely to tell them to go away, I meet a lot of freaks. I pulled the white cord to ring the bell when the bus approached my stop. Then I walked up the aisle to the front of the bus and waited for the driver to open the door.

"Edelweiss," the bus driver said, laughing once with a little snort.

After the doors shut behind me and the bus drove off, I realized he was making fun of my dress. I looked like I belonged in *The Sound of Music* or on a box of hot chocolate. This moment seared itself into my memory, the first in a long chain of shameful experiences that would be a result of wearing the IHOP uniform.

When I got back to Simplicity House after work, I told Irene, Jenny, and Gustavo the bus story in hopes of getting some sympathy. They laughed so hard they almost peed their pants. They'd calm down long enough for one of them to say *Edelweiss* and then the laughter would start all over again.

3

I FEEL LIKE the awkwardest, ugliest virgin of all time. I can't even think about how stupid I am, otherwise I want to slit the veins in the top of my feet and watch all the blood run into the matted beige carpet like a spilled soda. I used to ditch school every day so I could watch Hope on *Days of Our Lives*. When she and Bo got married, I was devastated. I kept trying to imagine myself instead of Bo with Hope on her honeymoon in that big fucking mansion. Hope looked like a beautiful virgin in her white dress. The hardest part to watch was when Bo carried her to bed and put her down so delicately, like she was his dog that accidentally ate a roach trap while he was at work.

Her big dying eyes looking into his, and his stupid chin jutting out, he'd say, "I thought the roach trap was farther behind the refrigerator, please don't die! Please don't die!"

Oh! I still get furious when I think about their wedding.

Sometimes I want to beat people's faces with stones. And then I get scared because I can't tell whether I thought, "I want to beat that person's face with a stone," or that it already happened, and I'd be holding the bloody stone with tingling hands, feeling light-headed and lost. Bo and Hope went to this estate for their honeymoon. There were tons of flowers and rare mosses everywhere. They spent the whole time walking around holding hands and barely talking. A Phil Collins song played in the background while they gave each other "meaningful" looks. The "meaningful looks" alluded to the fact that Hope was scared it would hurt to lose her virginity.

I'm a virgin and I'm not a virgin. I got rid of the ol' hymen if you know what I mean. I lost my virginity to a giant marking pen.

Eek, eek, that's the sound of marking pen writing on the page.

I love that squeak—the sound of something getting done.

Eek, eek, that's the sound I made when the marking pen went through my hymen.

I was hiding in my room because all these Marines were eating dinner at our house and I was sick of being a virgin, so I pushed the marking pen into my pussy, but it would only go so far. I stabbed harder, like I was trying to break up a frozen mass of ice, and finally my hymen broke. You know that ring on top of the pen that is supposed to hold the cap while you're writing? When I pulled the pen out of me after I broke my hymen, it was filled with hymen-skin. I'm not lyin', the ring was filled with hymen.

It sounds like a company jingle or bumper sticker, *I'm not lyin', it's filled with hymen.*

"Hope, when you lose your virginity it's the same as when a dog runs really fast and smacks into a screen door. The dog feels shock and some pain—a jolt maybe—but mostly it feels stupid and alone."

That's what I would have said if I could've talked to Hope before her honeymoon with Bo. Maybe it's different if Bo does it to you on your wedding night, than if you do it to yourself with a marking pen while the dining room is full of Marines. Maybe if Bo does it you don't feel humiliated afterward. I didn't exactly feel humiliated, in some ways I felt free, like I was in charge and happy. I was free, free, free—limping around the house by the time dessert came around. Free, free, free, with all the Marines eating bowls full of whipped cream. Did you know Marines like to eat only bowls full of whipped cream for dessert? There are a lot of Marines in my family. Some of them like cake and pie with their whipped cream, too. But whatever it is, Marines want extra.

"Extra jalapeños! Make it so hot my tongue burns off."

Then all the other Marines sit back and laugh, waiting for the other Marine to burn his tongue. One Marine gets out the video camera he bought when he was stationed in Okinawa and videotapes the other Marine shoveling a forkful of jalapeños into his mouth.

"It's always overkill with you. You don't know when to quit."

That's what my brother says to me.

Or he says, "Lighten up."

My brother and I were both children who repeated whatever our parents said, and my father always said, "It's always overkill with you."

One time someone tried to interview me for the school paper about my thoughts on prisoners' rights.

I said, "It's like a goddamned Club Med in there, with the TVs and steak for dinner."

My father had said the same thing weeks before.

When my family picked me up at the mental hospital, my brother said, "Why can't you just drink and not do drugs?"

My brother's kind of moderate. I'm more loud, flamboyant, and desperate. Whenever we moved somewhere new, my mom asked me to take my brother around to all the neighbors' houses and make friends for the both of us.

I wonder if Hope from *Days of Our Lives* is gay in real life. Oh my God, that would be so rad. She doesn't look gay, though.

I don't want to look like the person people think is the ugly dyke, with the short hair, flannel shirt, and no bra on. I could never go bra-less anyway. I've got big tits. In fact, my whole family has big tits and skinny calves. It's hard to believe a skinny-calf gene could be so powerful. My dad always used to tease my mom about her legs and say, "The last time I saw a leg that skinny it had a message tied to it."

I don't think I have gay hair, but I'm not sure. It comes down to the middle of my back and it's light brown. I want it to be messy like Janis Joplin's and most of the time I wear it under my backward black baseball cap that I got from the Tower Records free box. I'm medium height and kind of skinny, but only because I never have any money for food, not because I have a fast metabolism. When I turn sideways I can see my ribs. I have the kind of cheeks that people always pinch obnoxiously and say, "Awwww. Look at those cheeks." My whole life people have said I have puppy-dog eyes, too. My eyes are hazel and when I wear my dad's old army coat, my eyes turn exactly the same army green color. But I wear my black motorcycle jacket and combat boots every day.

When I told my parents I was gay and moving to San Francisco my dad said, "Good, now you can get a bunch of tattoos and look like a big dyke."

I laughed so hard when he said that. He laughed, too, and we both looked at each other, laughing so hard, as if it was a contest to see who could stand laughing in the kitchen with their mouth open the longest.

Then my mom said, "Tommmmm."

And there was the long pause of astonishment as if my father had tried to coerce a two-year-old to walk across hot coals.

The reason my dad knows what a lesbian looks like is because my brother's good friend, Kerry McAdams, has an older sister who ended up being gay. My dad ran into her at a soccer game her first year back from college. She sat in the bleachers with her girlfriend and watched her brother and my brother play soccer. The next day I went with my father to buy a new shirt for work.

We were parking the car in front of the store when he said, "Kerry McAdams's sister, Tracy, is a lesbian."

Just like that he said it. Out of the blue. As if he was saying, "Don't forget to roll up the window."

"How do you know she's a lesbian?" I asked, heart pounding excitedly.

"Because I saw her at the soccer game with her lesbian friend.

And the friend," he said with emphasis, "was obviously a lesbian. In fact, she might as well have been wearing a sandwich board that said 'lesbian' on it."

"Dad?" I asked tentatively.

"Yes."

"What's a sandwich board?"

"Do you learn anything in school?" my father steamed. "A sandwich board is the big wooden board that people wear over their shoulders to advertise something."

His voice was filled with disbelief at my ignorance.

"And that's exactly the kind of job you can look forward to if you don't crack the books," he finished.

Am I the only person in the world that found out what a sandwich board is after what a lesbian is? I could only imagine Tracy McAdams's girlfriend as a big butch dyke wearing a white sandwich board and sitting in the soccer field bleachers.

From that point on, whenever something happened that my father didn't like he'd say, "Good, go to San Francisco, and be a lesbian. You can get a bunch of tattoos and look like a truck driver. Or better yet, you can look like Tracy McAdams's girlfriend."

Initially my mother acted very composed when I told her I was gay. She thought all I needed was therapy. So two weeks later my mother, my father, and I went to one all-day emergency session with a man my mother had heard on the radio.

"How come Rich doesn't have to go?" I asked. "Doesn't he care about the family?"

"Your brother has to work," my mom answered.

The radiotherapist was late to our appointment and my father was muttering about paying all this money and the guy's late. When the radiotherapist finally showed up, my dad sized him up like they'd just met at a jukebox in a bar, and my dad didn't want to hear another Johnny Cash song. We all found places on his enormous black leather couch that wrapped around the room.

"So what brings you here?" the radiotherapist asked after shuffling a few papers on his desk.

"Well," my mother started, "Francesca, our daughter, thinks she's a lesbian and wants to move to San Francisco to live with one of her teachers from the community college."

The radiotherapist gazed out the window for a moment after my mother spoke and then asked lazily, "And that concerns you?"

"Humph. Yeah, I'd say I have a few concerns about that. Does that sound normal to you?"

"What about that doesn't seem normal to you?" the radiotherapist countered.

My mother was becoming annoyed. I think she'd assumed the therapist was always on the side of the homophobic parents.

"Well, as a mother, my first concern would be: why does the teacher have a shaved head? Why does this woman, who is obviously much older, hang out with her students? Why are students moving to San Francisco to live with their teacher? And if there's nothing 'weird' going on, why would Francesca be so adamant about us not meeting her, this teacher, with the shaved head?"

"They live two hours away!" I shouted.

Everyone in the room turned toward me. It was the first thing I'd said since we got there.

"How could they have met Irene when they live two hours away?" I asked the radiotherapist.

"We've always welcomed Francesca's friends into the home," my mom said quickly. "If this person is so important to her, why wouldn't she want us to meet her?"

The radiotherapist sunk into the couch with his expensive tennis shoes half-tied. It looked like he'd been up all night doing cocaine and having a three-way. He'd probably overslept and that was why he was late. I watched him stifle a yawn and tried to assess whether he had a big dick. He probably got a lot of ladies, being young, classically handsome, and rolling in it from Saturday sessions just like this one.

"Why can't you meet Irene now?" the radiotherapist finally said.

"Humph," my mom seethed.

He was really pissing her off.

"Meeting Irene at this point would be about as comfortable as fucking a goat," my mom said.

I laughed out loud.

"Jesus, Theresa," my father said.

"Well, that's exactly what it would be like," my mom said, her eyes tearing up.

I squealed with delight.

"That's an interesting way of putting it," the radiotherapist said.

"Really—I've never heard that before."

Actually, he didn't seem like he thought it was that interesting. My father picked the excess skin off his callused hands the way he does when he's irritated or nervous. No one said anything for a while. I tried to stifle my laughter every time I thought about what my mom had said. I was sure the radiotherapist was sorry he hadn't called in sick. I looked over at my mother, who was looking at my father for help. *About as comfortable as fucking a goat.* I loved my mother so much right then for saying that.

4

JENNY NAMED ME Goaty when I first arrived in San Francisco because I smelled so bad. I was petrified that environmentally conscious Irene would think I was a water waster so I abstained from showering at all. Sometimes if everyone was out of the house, I'd sneak in quickly, but there was barely a time I was alone between all of our schedules.

The first night I ate dinner with Irene, Jenny, and Gustavo, I volunteered to wash the dishes afterward. They do everything communally, even if it comes to slicing a tomato—someone will remove it from the refrigerator and hand it to someone who places it down on a cutting board that someone else washed, before the tomato even sees a knife.

Above Irene's sink is a handmade sign that says, *All work is meditation*. The sink holds two different Tupperware trays—one with clear water and one with soapy water from a jug of hippie soap.

"Instead of letting the water run indefinitely, Goaty, we fill these pans in the sink with water. When I move my hands over the dish, I clear my mind and try to be one with the Goddess."

I was used to washing dishes the American way: turn the faucet on high, get overwhelmed and distracted, and walk out of the room to watch the final round of *Jeopardy*. By the time one of the contestants had written down *Who is Karl Marx?* in a nervous scrawl,

I'd remember the open faucet and hear all the water rushing out furiously behind me.

My father has always been a proponent of the view that the only way to get things clean is to turn the water on so hot it almost burns your hands. He used to show us by darting his hands back and forth quickly under the scalding water.

"See," he'd say to us, "the water's hot. Make the water is as hot as you can stand it, and then scrub. Put some elbow grease into it."

His giant sun-speckled hands would nudge the faucet hotter and hotter as he put the tips of his fingers into the steaming water to test the temperature.

"You want the water so hot, you almost can't stand it. Hot water takes off grease. Cold water doesn't. Then you grab the sponge and scrub the shit out of it. This takes off all the food particles."

If my father had a handmade sign over the sink it would say, *Scrub the shit out of it.* We were taught to wash our faces in a similar fashion. Turn the water on hot, so it almost scalds you. Almost burn the shit out of your face and all the skin cells with it. Brushing our teeth required the same instructions. Select the toothbrush with the stiffest bristles. The proper way to brush teeth is to scrub and scrub and scrub. If our gums weren't bleeding at the end of a brushing, then we weren't trying our hardest. My father used to say about toothbrushes marked *soft* or *extra soft*, "That shit doesn't get teeth clean. You might as well be brushing your teeth with a goddamned feather pillow."

Needless to say, I felt confused when I looked at the two pans in Irene's sink waiting for me. *All work is meditation,* the sign kept reminding me. But as my hands moved from the pan of lukewarm soapy water to the pan of lukewarm clear water I knew deep down in my heart that the dishes weren't getting clean.

"I'm just going to add a little more hot water to the pan," I said to Irene when, even after careful insertion and extraction of the dish, I'd slopped all the water over the side.

Over my shoulder Irene seemed to be meditating, her eyes half-closed as she wiped the crumbs off the table with a damp rag.

"Sorry," I said, "I didn't mean to interrupt. I just have to add some more hot water."

She smiled benevolently and nodded.

"ALL WORK IS ULCER PRODUCING. That's what the sign should say," I whispered to Jenny, who'd come to dry the dishes.

"Oh, Goaty," she laughed.

I took the dirty dish and brought it down into the sink, carefully picking up a sponge and beginning to scrub the drying ratatouille off of it. When I dipped the sponge into the Tupperware basin, water went over the side and down the drain. It was a terrible feeling, looking at the remaining water in the basin and wondering if it would be enough to wash even one dish. Irene continued to brush crumbs from the table in silence. Since there was nothing for Jenny to dry so far, she wrapped the leftovers in some sort of biodegradable paper, unlike the awful plastic wrap that I'd been using my whole life. Gustavo separated the trash into what was recyclable and what was not. There was complete silence as we worked: Jenny, Gustavo, and Irene were *being* while I was racked with anxiety.

I've always hated washing the dishes and thought you had to joke around to make it tolerable. But my whole life has been frivolous joking. I want to practice nonviolence and be conscious like Irene.

After a dish was scrubbed, instead of rinsing under clear running water, it was supposed to be slid into the second Tupperware tray of clear water. The trays were so close together in the sink, however, that it was difficult not to drag the soap bubbles that were barely bubbles at all—due to their environmentally safe construction— from one tray into the other. There was also just enough room in the rinsing tray to fit the dish safely in and out. I felt my neck getting stiff, in the place it does when I become anxious. Irene sang a Sweet Honey in the Rock song under her breath and Jenny returned and stood patiently, waiting for the first dish to dry.

"What's wrong, Goaty?" she asked.

The mere fact of broken silence made me happy.

"I'm trying not to use all the water in the trays, because there isn't very much left. Sorry it's taking forever."

Irene looked across the kitchen at us, the shoulder strap of her faded red housedress dipping slightly down her arm. I wasn't sure if she was going to be upset that we were talking during meditative dish time.

"Goaty's afraid she's going to use up all the water in the trays," Jenny said on my behalf.

Irene smiled. "Goaty, if you use up all the water, we can fill the trays up again."

"You guys seem really good at not wasting water. I don't want to ruin everything."

"Well, we just don't leave the water constantly running because that's such an obvious waste of water," Irene said.

I was confused by the terminology, "obvious waste of water" and whether I was or was not "obviously wasting water." Jenny grabbed a towel and began to dry the only dish I had washed in the last ten minutes.

"I'll let you guys finish up in here," Irene said. "I've got to work at the health food store tomorrow, so Gustavo and I are going to practice some drumming in the other room before it gets too late."

Fine, go be with Gustavo, I fumed.

"Thanks for dinner," I hollered after her, "it was delicious."

The truth is that I'm really heartbroken by all these vegetable/gruel dishes, but when Irene makes them, they do taste good if you put all the little spicy sauces on top. Inevitably, everything ends up tasting like the spicy sauce because the meals are so bland.

After we heard Gustavo and Irene start jamming in the living room, Jenny and I began to talk.

"Goaty," Jenny said, "I'm so glad you're here. You make everything more fun. I want to be spiritual and meditate and everything. I'm really interested in that, but sometimes when Irene and Gustavo get together, they forget how to play."

"Do you feel like the Goddess is really watching us washing dishes?" I said.

"What do you mean?"

"All work is meditation," I said, pointing to Irene's hand-drawn sign that hung above the sink. "I mean, how does washing a fucking dish bring me closer to the Goddess?"

"It's just a concept, I guess. That if we have opportunities to clear our minds of all thoughts, and we can just be—" Jenny started.

"Just be what? Miserable," I interrupted. "Washing the dishes sucks. I'd rather think of anything besides the swirling motion of the sponge."

Jenny threw her arms around me and laughed, "I'm so glad you came up here, Goaty."

"But am I right about washing the dishes sucking?"

"Yeah. I'd rather dry than wash any day of the week."

Now that there was no pressure of running out of soapy or rinsing water, and Irene wasn't circling around in the background humming gospel songs, I moved quickly through the rest of the dishes, talking to Jenny about the new Peter Gabriel album.

Shortly after we were done Jenny went to bed because she had to get up at five in the morning for her job at Muffins Muffins. I was wide-awake so I lingered in the hallway, where Irene had stapled a giant piece of butcher paper to the wall. On it were quotes and pictures. I'd seen them when I first moved in, but I hadn't had time to really examine them because there was always someone hanging around. I leaned forward at a proof sheet of photographs and saw that they were tiny pictures of Gustavo and Irene. My heart started to turn that ugly brown when beautiful red meat first begins to cook in a pan. The pictures were more evidence against me. Against. Against because Gustavo was next to Irene in every photo while I was craning down examining them, wondering how to climb inside each frame to sit beside her. *What could I say* to make Irene throw her head back in simultaneous laughter and passion like she was in

the picture with Gustavo? *What could I say* to keep her head frozen
in that moment of joy?

Gustavo shaved Irene's head the first time and there are thirty-six
photographs to prove it. Various poses of Irene kneeling and Gustavo hovering over her patchy head with clippers—her looking sub-
missive and him like some nervous cult leader barber dressed in all
black with his grandfather's gold wire-rim glasses. Tall, lanky, dark-
eyed Gustavo with his own shaved head and goatee, with silver hoop
earrings in each of his ears.

"Faggot," teenage boys on the bus call him.

And he says nothing to correct them. It's his way of doing
activism for the rest of us. How fucking generous. If you really want
to do something to help, stop fucking the woman I love.

I paid special attention to the frames Irene had marked with a red
X. Were those ones to be enlarged?

Irene looking coy.

Irene running her hands through her newly shorn hair.

Irene in black panties and no shirt, stretching her arms over her head.

I felt nervous looking at pictures of my former philosophy
teacher topless.

Gustavo in his tiny gold spectacles looking pensive and serious.

Gustavo looking intense in a yard playing his drums.

*And Gustavo, head thrown back, laughing, like he knew the punch-
line to a joke I never would.*

The only photos of them together were a few of Gustavo shaving
Irene's head and a few of them sitting on a backyard staircase looking
like they'd recently had sex. Post-sex faces that were now ready to talk
about how to fix the areas in their life that were not utterly sacred.

Irene looked really sexy in the pictures where she was wearing
black panties and her head had just been shaved. I love Irene. I've
never been so in love in my life. The kind of love where you believe
if you can have the other person, everything will be perfect. Life will
be fine. Every drop of pain scrubbed free from life's sink.

5

BEFORE I MOVED to San Francisco to be with Irene, I was renting my childhood room from *the people*. *The people* moved into the house I grew up in when my parents moved out. They just so happened to be my childhood babysitter, Susie Broil, and her sometimes-recovering alcoholic husband who could never hold a job. They loved to watch TV programs like *COPS* and *Real Life Limbs Torn from Body* and *Dumb Asses Buy Recreational Vehicles, Get Drunk, and Almost Die.* The sometimes-recovering alcoholic husband was nice if you weren't married to him. Sometimes we went to AA meetings together.

When I lived with *the people,* I watched the movie *Camille Claudel* obsessively. Camille Claudel was the lover of the famous sculptor Rodin. She was a sculptor, too, but the movie is about how she totally got fucked over by him. She was poor and had no money for art supplies, so in the middle of the night she'd dig up clay from the wet ground with her sister.

In one scene Camille Claudel has this big art show, her one chance to prove to the world she's a real artist. But right before the show, she gets into a lovers' quarrel with Rodin—she gets pregnant with his baby but he makes her have an abortion. Then she shows up drunk to the opening with all this crazy white mime makeup on her face and wanders around the gallery spilling champagne and making crass remarks. Nobody at the show likes her art. They can't tell she's brilliant because they're idiots.

A few weeks later her studio is filled with various incomplete sculptures of Rodin. She's trying to sculpt his face from memory. The camera pans over the mounds of wet clay to her body lying facedown in a few inches of water. For a second you think she's dead. All her cats are circling her body. But she isn't dead—she's just passed out drunk in her flooded apartment. She lives. Only to make some sort of comeback in the art world and get back together with Rodin. She has two seconds of happiness until he shuns her for good. She has a nervous breakdown and gets institutionalized, complete with an ice-pick lobotomy. I loved to cry at the devastating ending.

That's what I want my writing to do—send an ice pick right through the reader's brain. I want Irene to feel so bleak and devastated when she reads one of my poems that she falls in love with me.

* * *

For a book titled *The IHOP Papers* I sure haven't told you much about IHOP. I'd only worked at IHOP for a month before I was promoted from hostess to waitress.

Julio said, "We're going to train you for waitress, okay? You'll still hostess sometimes, too, but mostly you'll be a waitress."

"I don't want to get promoted," I answered, "please don't do that to me."

I was really nervous. I mean really, really, nervous. I was sure I'd never be able to carry all those plates on my arms, but at the same time I wanted to be the best waitress ever. I wanted to be so graceful that people would have to stop eating and stare astounded as I glided through the dining room with plates stacked from my wrists to my shoulders.

Two weeks after I started waitressing, a really pregnant woman sat in my section and ordered a bowl of soup. Pregnant customers always try to guilt-trip you. I learned that right away.

"Tell the kitchen to rush this order, please. I'm pregnant and I feel like I'm going to pass out if I don't eat immediately."

Allergy people are the same way. It's hard to tell who is lying and who is telling the truth.

"If there is *even one green pepper* ground up in the sauce, I could die," says the allergy person.

I always say, "Really?" in the most disinterested voice I can muster or, "Oh, you don't have to worry about green peppers. There certainly aren't any real vegetables in a two-mile radius of this restaurant."

If they're so close to death, why are they eating at IHOP in the first place?

Bo from *Days of Our Lives* would probably be an allergy customer. Or worse. He'd impregnate Hope and then bring her in and be the crazy spawn father.

"My wife has had a difficult pregnancy and needs to get her meal right away, otherwise the baby's health could be jeopardized," Bo would say.

Then Hope would shoot him a mean glare and look totally embarrassed to be eating with such an insensitive boor.

"Please don't trouble the kitchen. You can bring it whenever it's ready," she'd say.

And then in a voice that sounded big sister to Bo but implied deep lust and sexual curiosity to me, "You look adorable in that dress and you have the cutest cheeks."

After taking the order, I'd return to the kitchen and tell the cooks to rush her meal but to take a long, long time with Bo's.

At IHOP, the waitstaff is responsible for making soups and

salads. It's the only food that doesn't come out of the kitchen. Under the soup and salad station, there is a little refrigerator where the extra six-gallon plastic containers of dressings are kept. On top of the salad-dressing refrigerator are the vats of soup. Every night we serve beef barley soup and a daily special soup. For example, Tuesday is potato cheddar soup, Wednesday is clam chowder, and Thursday is vegetable soup. But the truth is there are only two kinds of soup, the cream based and the water based.

"What soup do we have tonight?" a waitress will ask at the beginning of her shift.

Another waitress will open the lid, squint, and say, "It's either clam chowder or potato cheddar."

Or, "It's either vegetable or minestrone."

Even after tasting it, half the time the soup's true identity remains a mystery.

"I think it's the potato one."

"No, I'm pretty sure that was a clam."

"Was it?"

"Huh, now I'm not sure."

"Well, it's either a clam or a solidified piece of cheddar," one of us will say, nudging the solidified globule with a ladle.

Actually we only have one soup. Salt soup. There is so much salt in all our soup, it's all you can taste.

Molly always says, "Salt. The silent killer."

I laughed so hard the first time she said that. Then she said it at least twelve times each shift and it wasn't funny anymore.

She'd follow me around and whisper in my ear, "Salt, the silent killer."

Molly doesn't care what she says to a customer.

One time this man came in after having oral surgery and mumbled, "Cun you rekmend sumfin? I jist had four teef pulled."

Molly said, "Oh you poor thing. Let me get you a bowl of beef barley to gargle with, its high salt content will prevent infection."

Or . . .

"What kind of soup do you have tonight?"

"Petrified salt carrot."

Molly is fucking funny. But sometimes she scares me. She talks a lot of shit behind people's backs.

It's a pain in the ass to get soup, salad, or hot tea for a customer. You have to assemble a meal instead of just picking a plate up from under the heat lamp. Putting a doily on top of a plate and then setting a spoon next to it, or getting a lemon wedge and coaster for a customer, is psychologically exhausting. But nothing is as bad as making an ice-cream sundae. The ice cream is so old and hard, it's like trying to scoop a sundae from a headstone and the whipped cream cans are usually flat because Tim and Kirsten suck the gas out of them to get high. I forget my coworkers are primarily drug addicts until it's too late and I end up spraying flat whipped cream on a sundae. It's a disgusting sight, runny cream dripping over the ice cream. Then you have to make the sundae all over again, the whole time hating Tim or Kirsten or whatever graveyard Goth employee who couldn't afford real drugs sucked the whipped cream cans dry.

We store a plastic bin of crackers and a backup box of crushed walnuts for ice-cream sundaes on a glass shelf above the soup and salad station. One day a really pregnant woman was sitting at table 32, which is the booth directly behind the salad bar, and ordered a bowl of clam chowder. It sucks when anyone sits at table 32 because it's right next to where Molly and I hide to gossip, make fun of The Big Boss, and ravenously eat salad bar croutons.

"Make sure the soup's hot. If it's not hot I'll send it back," the really pregnant woman threatened.

"Touché," I said, walking away.

I love when people say to make sure the soup is hot because then I can put it in the microwave until it bubbles up into a boiling, festering, sore.

"It's microwave time," I said to Molly, ladling the soup into a white bowl.

It takes nothing to get Molly excited about ruining other people's lives. She smiled evilly, grabbed the bowl from my hand, put it in the microwave, and punched in three minutes. After thirty seconds, a bowl of soup is steaming. A minute passed and it bubbled and boiled over the edge of the white bowl.

"I hope it burns her frickin' windpipe and goes straight into the womb and scalds her little fetus's forehead," Molly said.

My brain flashed on images of graphic anti-abortion posters, but I couldn't help but laugh.

"She's a frickin' bitch. We'll make her frickin' soup hot," Molly ranted.

The bowl turned in circles inside the microwave. I was beginning to feel scared by the bubbling volcanic mess. When the timer went off, I reached for the microwave door but Molly blocked my way, punching in another three minutes.

"Jesus, Molly."

She crossed her arms and stood in front of me, daring me to try and stop her.

"Molly. God. Take it out. She'll never eat that."

There was practically no soup left in the bowl, it had bubbled all over the paper coaster and the bottom of the microwave, gurgling up like a broken drain.

"Go get crackers and a spoon," Molly ordered.

I walked over to the soup and salad station and reached into the plastic bin for the pregnant lady's crackers. Suddenly, I felt dizzy, unsteady. Then I realized I wasn't moving—the cracker bin had toppled off the shelf towards the really pregnant lady sitting on the other side of the soup and salad station partition. The cracker bin holds approximately five hundred individually wrapped pairs of crackers. These were now scattered all over table 32 and her lap. Suddenly feeling terrible for her, I came careening out from behind the soup and salad station to her booth.

"Look what you *did to me*," the pregnant lady whined.

"I'm so sorry," I said. "The box just slid off the shelf."

"Obviously, the box slid off the shelf, Einstein," she snapped.

My face burned. I didn't know what to do, so I knelt down and started to pick the crackers up, one by one, off the ground. I could feel the bubble of stretched-out pantyhose hanging between my legs as I squatted over the crackers. My ankles were frozen from the air conditioner. IHOP purposely cranks it up, so customers won't get too comfortable, sitting around socializing, taking up table space after their meals are finished.

"Fran-ces-ca. Are you stupid?"

It was the voice of The Big Boss.

"The box slid off the shelf," I tried to explain.

"I didn't ask you if the box slid off the shelf," he said. "I asked if you were stupid. How could you let a box of crackers fall on this pregnant lady?"

I got up off the carpet and put the handful of crackers back into the plastic bin. Molly came over to help me pick up the crackers. I felt like quitting right there on the spot.

"He's such a frickin' douche bag," she whispered.

The Big Boss walked over to the cash register and got out a One Free Dinner Entrée gift certificate for the pregnant lady. This is his answer to any customer complaint. After the customer leaves, he threatens to make whoever fucked up pay for the cost of the customer's meal. As if IHOP can't cover a free meal.

I always want to say, "One Free Dinner Entrée isn't money. It's a piece of construction paper that you give people so they can come in and eat the worst meal of their life as some sort of twisted compensation for eating the worst meal of their life."

But The Big Boss scares me so I don't say anything. We call him The Big Boss because he isn't. He's a glorified host that orders the same baked chicken dinner every night as his employee meal.

Once Molly said, "I paid Enrique five dollars to piss on The Big Boss's chicken tonight. And he did it."

"You're lying," I said.

But immediately I knew she wasn't.

"The Big Boss ate every bite, too."

The Big Boss has a ritual of chain-smoking over his half chicken for a good five minutes before he starts to eat it. Molly watches him from around the corner, waiting for him to accidentally ash on his dinner, and then unknowingly eat it. If he does, she reports it triumphantly.

6

A FEW WEEKS after I arrived in San Francisco Jenny and Gustavo got into a big fight. I came home from an AA meeting and Irene looked at me somberly and said that Gustavo had punched Jenny in the stomach during a fight.

"He punched her?" I asked outraged. "That's intentionally abusive. I hope you're kicking him out of the house."

I could tell it was a struggle for Irene to take a stand against Gustavo. After Gustavo punched Jenny, he ran out of the house and Irene was now waiting for him to return. Jenny went to a café to calm down, so she wouldn't be there when Gustavo came back. She was going to let Irene handle it. After all, Irene was the one who taught a class called the Philosophy of Non-Violence.

"We're going to have a big talk about things when Gustavo gets back," Irene said. "He's probably cooling off right now, taking a walk, and soon he'll be back, ready to apologize, like he always does after he acts out."

I hate the expression *act out*.

"You're probably going to want to stay out of the house for a while, Goaty. I don't think it's going to be too pleasant around here when Gustavo comes back."

I'd already been out most of the day. First, I'd worked at IHOP and then I went to an AA meeting, walking there and back. After the meeting I'd been too shy to talk to anyone. I sat there eating generic cookies and drinking instant coffee while rescinding on the promise I made to myself to stay and make friends, extend my hand to another alcoholic. I darted away out the door and down Mission Street, smoking as soon as I had my foot on the sidewalk.

In minutes it was freezing, the fog and wind had eaten up the sun. All the way up Van Ness Street, I kept looking over my shoulder for the bus. When I saw its orange top approaching, I couldn't decide if I wanted to spend the dollar or not. *I'm almost home. Just keep going.* My hand was numb from holding cigarette after cigarette in the cold and I had a headache. I was happy to be gone from Simplicity House all day, convinced that after twelve hours, Irene would feel my absence. I wanted to curl up and cuddle with Jenny—break Simplicity House's no-sugar rule and eat Twinkies hidden from Irene. Instead Jenny was at a café recovering from being punched.

"Call in a couple hours to check in," Irene said. "I know how you hate being around conflict."

"Okay," I sulked, turning to go out the door I'd just come in.

"Where will you go?" Irene asked.

I saw a look of concern for me in her eyes and seized the opportunity to exploit it.

"Don't worry. I'll find somewhere to sleep."

"But where? You don't know anyone in San Francisco."

"I'll figure it out."

There was practically a spring in my step as I ran down the stairs back to the cold street. It would be so easy to sleep at Maria's house. *She's my sponsor.* As soon as I tell her Gustavo punched Jenny she'll beg me to come over. If domestic violence wasn't a cause to sleep at your sponsor's house, what was?

The closest pay phone I knew was in a bus shelter four blocks from Simplicity House. I walked there quickly and inside I pulled out my AA schedule, where Maria had written her phone number. I dug out some change that was mixed with loose tobacco from the bottom of my backpack, and my heart pounded as I dialed her number.

"Ummm, hi, Maria. This is Francie from AA. I'm sitting in this bus stop because Irene's boyfriend punched her girlfriend and there's all this drama. Let me give you the number of the pay phone here. 675-7754. I was wondering if I could maybe sleep at your house tonight because I don't know anyone else in San Francisco. It's totally cool if I can't. There's totally no pressure. I'll just sit at the bus stop and wait for you to call back. Hope you're good. Bye."

Suddenly I felt perplexed. I hadn't anticipated her answering machine picking up. The adrenaline that had launched me out of the house at the prospect of seeing Maria had completely dissipated and fatigue took its place as I slid down the plastic wall of the bus shelter onto the cold concrete. Occasionally people came into the shelter to wait for the bus. Most avoided looking me in the eye. They thought I was homeless because I was sitting inside the bus shelter chain-smoking. I was starting to feel a little homeless waiting for Maria's call. Irene was right—where would I sleep since I didn't know anyone in San Francisco? But there was no way I was going to swallow my pride and go back to Simplicity House. Let Irene nurture Gustavo and Jenny tonight.

Finally I was alone in the bus shelter, and I pulled my small blue paper box of razor blades out of my motorcycle jacket. I knew one good way to pass the time. I tried to push the sleeve of my leather jacket up, but it was too stiff. If I didn't care about having scars on my hands, then I could slash them up and still stay warm. But there's no way I can serve food with mental-hospital hands. Reluctantly, I unzipped my jacket and slipped one arm out into the freezing cold. I pushed my T-shirt sleeve up and saw the fresh pink slashes on my shoulder from my stint in the airport bathroom before I flew to San Francisco. I halfheartedly hacked at my shoulder. It's hard to draw blood when you're cold because all the skin cells are constricted, but when I cut myself after a warm bath, there's a lot of blood. I like to let myself bleed for a bit and then lay my T-shirt sleeve over the cuts like a bandage. When the sleeve dries stuck to my arm, I can rip it off and all the cuts scar better. I really know how to throw a party. At the bus stop I hacked unsuccessfully for a while, my stomach bunching up into knots at the lousy results. I needed to bring Maria proof that I'd had a hard night. With that in mind, I swung my hand hard, but the silver tip of the razor left a weak dotted slash. Out of the corner of my eye I saw a guy walking toward the bus stop, so I slipped my arm back inside my jacket sleeve and felt the sting of the failed slashes.

"Can I bum a cigarette?" he asked.

I handed him one, trying to look as tough as I could.

I had no idea what time it was, but the once-regular flow of people who'd been at the bus stop didn't exist now.

"I've got all this scrap metal hidden over on Eddy Street and I was going to take it down to SOMA and then buy a bag. You wanna get high with me?" he said.

Was he picking up on me?

"No, thanks."

I looked at his filthy fingernails as he held the cigarette.

"You look like you know how to party. We can get at least one bag from all this metal," he mumbled, lingering in the bus shelter with me in silence.

I kept smoking, trying to watch him out of the corner of my eye in case he tried to make a sudden lunge to rape or kill me. My shoulder was stinging from where I'd cut it. Thankfully the pay phone rang and I scrambled off the concrete to answer it.

"Francie?"

"Hi."

"Sorry I missed your call, I was on a date and we just got home."

We? My heart sank.

"No, I'm sorry to bother you. I just didn't know who else to call."
"I can buy us a bag after I sell this metal—" the guy said to me.
"Back the fuck up," I yelled.
"Who are you talking to?" Maria asked.
"Don't even ask. I'll tell you about it later."
"Come over. I'll make you a little bed on the floor of the living room, okay?"
"I owe you one," I said in my best tough-guy voice after she gave me her address.
When I hung up the phone the creepy guy was still looking at me.
"Have fun with your bag," I said.
"I'll walk with you. Where are you going?" he continued cluelessly. I ignored him. According to the map on the bus shelter wall, I figured it would take me two to three hours to walk to Maria's house. She lived way past the Mission in the Excelsior District and I was in Pacific Heights. While I was looking at the map I heard the creepy guy begin to roll his shopping cart of scrap metal away from me.
"Well, you don't have to be such a stuck-up bitch," he muttered.
I was gonna wait forever for a bus at this time of night. I considered taking a cab. I'd never taken a cab in my life. Now it seemed like they were everywhere, speeding down streets and piled up on curbs in front of coffee shops. I counted the change in the bottom of my backpack. $1.47. How much did cabs cost, anyway? I walked up to one and knocked on the window. The driver was reading the newspaper. He rolled down the window.
"Can you take me $1.47 of the way to 3423 Chattanooga?" I asked, reading him the address off my hand.
He paused for a moment before saying, "Ahhh, get in. I'm slow tonight anyway."
I hadn't realized how cold I was until I got in and felt the blast of warmth from the car heater. The clock on his dashboard told me I'd been sitting at the bus stop waiting for Maria's call for over two and

a half hours. We drove past all the buildings I'd walked past on the way to IHOP and on the way home from the AA meeting.

Fifteen minutes later the cab jerked over to the curb. We'd arrived.

"Here you go," he said.

I leaned forward and started to hand him the $1.47.

"Thanks so much."

"Don't worry about it."

Then he noticed the money.

"Keep your money," he said.

"Thanks again," I said, getting out and walking up to the apartment door.

Maria's porch was dark. I felt around anxiously for a doorbell. I was nervous about seeing her. Then the door opened and the light went on. Maria appeared, wearing a black dress and her bright-red lipstick. I wanted to throw my arms around her and bury my nose into her perfumed neck, but I couldn't move.

"I hope I didn't ruin your date," I lied, standing fixed to the porch.

"Shut up," she teased, pulling me tightly toward her and escorting me into the house.

When we walked into the kitchen my eyes settled on Maria's tall butch date leaning against the counter.

"Hi, I'm Ashanti," the date said.

"I'm Francie," I said, extending my hand. "Sorry to interrupt your date."

"No, not at all," Ashanti said.

"Let me show you your bed," Maria said, taking my hand and leading me to the living room.

Her hand felt so incredible in mine at that moment, I would've followed her right over a cliff. On the floor were two neatly folded blankets, one for the mattress and one for the blanket, surrounded by glowing red votive candles.

"Oh, it's so beautiful," I said.

"I thought you might like candles after your hard night."

"I didn't have anyone else to call."

"So what happened?"

Maria's perfume was an intoxicating blend of citrus. I wanted her to sit on the floor next to the little bed she'd made me, and hold my hand the way she did when she led me from the kitchen into the little room. I wanted to be on a date with Maria right now.

"Tell me what happened."

"I don't even know where to begin," I said. If I seemed mysterious and injured would she stay next to me longer?

"Basically, Gustavo just punched Jenny in the stomach," I said, looking into her green eyes.

"God. Men should just be swept from the face of the earth. All they do is abuse women, start wars, and rape women."

Then she laughed out loud.

"Well, it's true," Maria added, smiling.

Suddenly I remembered my razor wounds and took off my leather jacket. I positioned myself so that my cut-up shoulder faced her. For a second, my eyes caught hers. When I heard Ashanti moving around in the kitchen, I looked away self-consciously.

"Are you really okay?" she asked.

I nodded.

"I should go back to my date."

"Of course. I'm sorry."

"Stop saying sorry. I'll see you in the morning," she said, bending over to hug me.

"Thanks for everything," I said, holding on to her as long as I could.

After much tossing and turning and trying to hear Ashanti and Maria having sex through the wall, I fell asleep. The glowing red candles and pungent burning wick smoke followed me into my dream. I was trying to walk to the bathroom. I staggered drunkenly in a red-lit haze, trying to find my way down the hall to Maria's bedroom, but I kept stumbling and bumping into things. Finally, Maria came out of her bedroom and I tried to talk, but it was impossible to do so without slurring. I kept saying, "I'm not drunk, I'm not drunk." All night, I woke up panicked by different dreams. But when I fell back asleep, I picked up in the exact place I'd left off before.

When morning came I woke to find Maria holding a phone out to me.

"Irene's on the phone for you."

"Irene?"

I took the phone from Maria, not quite awake.

"Hello?"

"Hi, Goaty. We had a hard night, but it's okay. You can come home now. Gustavo understands what he's done and he's going to stay living here. Under the conditions of course that if this ever happens again, he's out the door."

I watched Maria walk from the sink to the coffee pot in a red slip.

"How'd you find me?" I asked.

"I remembered your sponsor's name and looked her up in your phone book," Irene said proudly.

Maria walked back into the room, holding a cup of coffee out to me, her breasts exposed slightly under her red slip. My heart raced as I took the cup of coffee from her hands. She was so unbelievably sexy.

"Are you there, Goaty?" Irene said.

"Sorry. I'm not quite awake yet."

"Come on home, Goaty. I miss you. Everything's okay now," Irene assured me.

7

AFTER ABOUT A month of living with Irene, Jenny, and Gustavo, I moved into my own apartment at 938 Geary Street in the Tenderloin. It smells like old carpet and roach powder, but in a good way. Bill, the super, had told me when I moved in not to worry about the white and green powder that was sprinkled around the edges of the apartment.

"Boric acid," he hollered, "covers all the pores in the roaches' bodies so they suffocate and die. Don't worry, though, it's not toxic."

Bill's a chain-smoking recovering alcoholic. When I had to go into his apartment to fill out the rental application, it was lunchtime. He was heating up some canned spaghetti and his longhaired cats were walking dangerously close to the simmering pot on the stove.

"I carry a gun right here," he said, patting the inside of his green army coat. "There's no bullshit in my building."

I think I only got the apartment since after he volunteered he was in AA I told him I was in AA, too. He pushed the door open to show me the vacant apartment, and the bottom of the door snagged on the uneven carpet. Then he lit up a cigarette in my new apartment. It was well lit and the biggest studio I'd seen. I was going to have my own apartment—one rectangular room with a kitchen behind it and a bathroom, all for $395 a month.

I don't know why they call it the Tenderloin, but that's the name of my neighborhood. It isn't a pretty place, except for some of the diners. It seems like it might get depressing after a while because of all the drug addicts and prostitutes walking around, and right in front of my door there's all these homeless guys who sleep in boxes. I've only met two of them. The nice one is Andy and the mean one is Mark.

I moved into my apartment after working a Sunday brunch shift at IHOP. Roxanne, my speed-freak coworker, helped me pick up all my boxes at Irene's house and drove me to my apartment. I wanted Irene to come with me but she was helping Gustavo make an outline for his research paper. It was really nice of Roxanne to help me, since we barely know each other. She double-parked, shuttled my few boxes from the trunk to the sidewalk outside my front gate, and then screeched off. I dragged them into the elevator, totally afraid that someone was going to get mad at me for tying up the elevator.

Once I got all my boxes inside my apartment, I unpacked, put my toothbrush in the built-in ceramic toothbrush holder over the sink, and filled the tub. Then I stared at myself in the full-length mirror. I couldn't believe that I'd actually gone and gotten my labia pierced. It was so fun taking people's orders later that day, knowing I had a ring in my pussy.

"Such a nice girl," the senior citizens crooned as I went away to get their coffee, a sharp tingle radiating between my legs.

After a long time of looking at myself in the mirror and spacing out, I remembered the water running in the bath. The tiles around the bathtub are the size of dimes but square. As I stepped into the tub I noticed the water looked green. I looked around the bathroom trying to find out what was reflecting green. Then I reached for the soap and realized I'd forgotten to buy any, so I leaned back, defeated, into the hot water. I heard the neighbors screaming at each other through the wall.

"Shut the fuck up! Shut up!" a woman shrieked.

"Stop busting my balls!" a man shouted back.

I was afraid the fight would escalate into one of them shooting the other.

Why was the water so green? I turned the faucet on to see if it was really the water or just the reflection from the fluorescent ceiling lamp. The water from the faucet was clear. There was nothing to even reflect green in the bathroom. Then I saw lines of white and green boric acid around the edges of the tub. The roach detergent. I was soaking in it.

8

WHEN I LIVED with *the people* every week I cut out the same classified ad for a lesbian and bisexual women "rap group" in Hollywood held on Sundays from 3 to 5 P.M. in a church basement. I felt excited when I thought about going to it, even though I've always been put off by the name "rap group." What kind of lesbians would show up for a "rap group"? Would punk girls with beautiful clavicles be there? Would the teacher with the shaved head and the giant German Expressionist hands be there? No, she would not. She moved to San Francisco into Simplicity House with two of her former students who were now her lovers. I knew I had to go to San Francisco to be with her but I never expected to end up at IHOP.

* * *

Today I filled in during the day shift and got to work with this really nice girl, Lan, who helped me practice carrying all the plates. She also told me she hides her tip money in a hole in her apartment wall.

"That way my boyfriend doesn't know how much money I have, and I can't waste my tips shopping."

"You just drop your tips into a hole?" I asked incredulously. "How do you know where it is inside the wall?"

"I take everything I don't need for bills, fold it up, put it in a sock and then drop it in the hole. The inside of the wall is hollow so if you ever need money you can make another hole at the bottom of the wall to get it out.

"You're lying," I said, trying to imagine the inside of her walls filled with money-stuffed socks.

"We all do it," said Tobie.

"But what about the holes?" I asked. "Won't the super get mad you're cutting holes in the wall?"

"Just spackle it before you move out. Until then, put a picture over the hole so no one knows it's there."

"But what if you can't find the money?" I said.

"You can't miss it. It's right at the bottom of the wall. And if you get robbed, no one will ever look in the wall. We've been robbed so many times, but they only got my cheap jewelry. I put my good jewelry in the wall, too."

Lan said the hole should be the size of a lemon.

"You don't want the hole to be so big that anyone could put their hand into the wall and fish out the money. And always make sure you drop at least one dollar in quarters, so it's heavy enough to hit the floor."

I couldn't decide how to make the hole exactly but decided the best way would be to just swing a hammer. I put a sock on the end of the hammer to try and muffle the sound and then I tried to swing it at the wall, but I didn't have the courage to swing it really hard at first. I didn't even dent the wall. It felt like when I try to cut myself and can't get the momentum of my hand going fast enough to get a real deep cut and then I just have some piddly little scratch. But by the third time, the hammer made a hole and I heard the plaster fall down inside the wall. I also thought I heard some kind of scurrying sound, but I was probably just being paranoid. I folded up two twenty-dollar bills and four singles, put four quarters on top, put it all in a sandwich bag, and then twisted a tie around the top. I hesitated a moment before I dropped it, afraid it might fall six stories down, but then I pushed the baggie full of money into the wall and the coins clinked as they hit the base of the floor like Lan said they would.

This felt way more exciting than just depositing money in the bank. I felt like one of those old recluses eating cat food for dinner who had a million dollars hidden in their house. It won't be long before I'm eating cat food on my own private island. I tried to decide what picture I could use to cover the hole. I decided on one of the photos I took of Irene for my photo assignment. It's a closeup of her lying on a grave in a cemetery. Her eyes are closed and the sun is illuminating her crow's-feet. You can't see the grave. The picture is just a closeup of her face with her giant beautiful eyes closed. I pushed a thumbtack into each corner of the photo, and just like Lan said, no one would be able to know there was a hole in the wall.

After I dropped the money into the wall, I realized I forgot to keep money out to buy cigarettes. Lan said she deposits everything but five dollars a day. I put everything in because I want to save as much as I can, as fast as I can. I'm going to keep the bare minimum I need for rent and bills in my regular checking bank account, but the money in the wall will be my savings.

The only thing that worries me is if rats in the wall eat my tips. Lan said a lot of rats live in old buildings like ours and if you can hear them crawling around all the time, then you have to open up the wall and check, because rats eat anything. That seems terrifying. Once Lan lived in this apartment building that had such a bad rat problem that she couldn't get rid of them no matter what she tried. This old lady told her to make balls of raw hamburger with ground-up glass inside and then to drop the hamburger into the wall. The rats eat the hamburger and then die because the glass rips up their intestines.

I was horrified. How do people figure things like this out?

"But doesn't the wall smell like dead rats and rotting hamburger?" I asked.

"That's better than them eating your hard-earned money. Anyway, if it smells you can just light a bunch of candles and buy potpourri."

I think I'd rather have rats eat my life savings than trick them into ripping up their intestines. That doesn't sound very nonviolent to me.

9

THE OFFICIAL IHOP Employee Contract states that an IHOP employee is prohibited from wearing necklaces or rings (with the exception of a wedding/engagement set). In addition, female employees can't have more than one earring in each earlobe and male employees can't wear earrings at all, or have beards. It doesn't say whether or not female employees are allowed to have beards. Female employees can't have fingernails longer than half an inch, wear nail polish unless it's a neutral tone, or have charm accessories attached to the fingernail. I had never considered a gold charm hanging off my pinky, until I read the manual.

I spend forty hours a week in my IHOP uniform. My only social outings are AA meetings. When I'm working as a hostess, I stand at the extremely shiny chrome register next to The Big Boss and ring up customers' checks. My other duty as a hostess is to distribute customers evenly around the restaurant who will then be waited on by an assortment of drug addict IHOP coworkers. Often I'm famished.

Meals are not free for IHOP employees—instead, they are half-price. We aren't allowed to eat mistakes either, because The Big Boss thinks we will make mistakes on purpose so we can eat for free.

Sometimes I'll notice a short stack of pancakes under the heat lamp for twenty minutes, and after I make sure no one's around, very casually I'll pick it up like I'm going to deliver it to a customer. Instead, I hide in the corner by the coffee pot and shove an entire pancake into my face, trying to chew inconspicuously as I refill the Sweet and Low containers.

I'm not the only one constantly hungry. Lan hides pancakes in her pockets and then tears off pieces when no one is looking and pops them in her mouth like Valiums. The first time I saw her pull a ball of navy-blue lint off a pancake, I was horrified because all I could think about was how I wouldn't want to eat anything that had touched something that smelled as bad as my dress. It smells like a sweaty armpit covered in syrup. But now I hide food in my pockets, too. Our pockets are really big because we have to keep so much in them, like our grease pencils, ticket books, and extra straws.

* * *

Almost all the guys who work at IHOP have AIDS. Darrel, the graveyard manager, is really sick. He almost died in the hospital a week ago. Everyone but Molly went and visited him. It's so sad because he's only twenty. The only guys who don't have AIDS are William, Julio, and The Big Boss. On my first day at IHOP, Tim told me he was one of the first people ever to be recorded as having AIDS. Everyone hates working with Tim because he's such a rage-a-holic despite the fact that he takes three Valiums before every shift. He says, "Fucking Julio," no matter what happens. Like if Molly didn't fill her sugar bowl after the day shift, he'll say, "Fucking Julio didn't check if Molly did her side work. Now I have to do her side work and my own fucking side work."

He slams anything capable of making a loud bang: doors, plates, the lid to the soup vat. Even when it isn't busy, he finds something to get upset about. His face gets so distorted when he's angry and he looks insane because he's wearing the big black IHOP bow tie and white shirt. He's like a demented Good Humor ice-cream man you'd encounter when you were on acid. Shit like that used to happen to me all the time when I was on acid.

I'm the only person Tim likes. Probably because I just sit around quietly while he slams things. People always think I'm on their side, because I'm too depressed or scared to tell them I'm not.

10

ABOUT AN HOUR before my ride to the airport picked me up to move to San Francisco, I sliced my arms in the bathroom at home. When I got to the airport I repeated the cutting in the bathroom there, because once I was in San Francisco I'd be standing before Irene for the first time with her knowing I loved her. I was moving to be near her—she'd said come—but when I'd finally get to her door, Gustavo and Jenny would be there with her, too. They'd be a family and I would not be a part of it. I was thinking all this when I carved my arms, pausing to stare at my sad eyes in the mirror at home. And later at the airport I worked quietly in the stall, hacking quickly, until an aching throb surrounded each bloody stripe. When I got a good cut, the slash would turn white where the skin separated and then the blood would come pouring out. When I get a good cut I like to hold my arm straight out from my body and then lower it slowly so that the stream of blood can curl around my arm with the same delicate precision I want to trail the tip of my nose down Irene's neck and across her collarbones.

For almost a year before Irene moved to San Francisco I'd loved her passionately, secretly—acting the part of the good, listening, friend. We sat in coffee shops until the wee hours, me staring hard at my boots and trying to look tough while she talked about her need to live simply. When it was time to leave, I always fell into a terrible depression and said I felt like killing myself. Every parting from Irene was pure devastation.

"I don't know how I'm going to go on. How can I go on? How? How?"

Irene would hold me in her car for an hour and I'd bury my face into her thick sweater, only coming up when I needed air. Despite all this, she had no idea I was in love with her. Instead, she thought I was severely depressed and my midnight outbursts were a side effect of that. While certainly this was true, the parallel truth was I was tortured by my obsession with her. I would invent things so I could hang out with her, asking her to pose for my photography assignments or show up during her office hours and talk about Nietzsche.

And when we were hanging out, I would invent reasons to extend our meetings even longer. Usually I tried to sound desperate and suicidal, which always won her sympathy.

"Have you ever lifted your tongue up when you're brushing your teeth and seen those purple veins under there?"

"Yeah," she'd say, lifting her eyebrow inquisitively.

"Well, I've always wanted to slit those veins with a razor and see if the blood spurts up on the ceiling."

Like clockwork, Irene would say to me, "Do you still want to stay in the car a little longer and talk a bit?"

One night after watching a movie at Irene's apartment with a bunch of other students from our Philosophy of Nonviolence class, Irene walked us outside to say good night. Everyone left, but I lingered next to Irene as the last student's truck screeched out of the apartment complex parking lot.

"Goodnight, sweetie," Irene said, moving to hug me.

No.

No leaving.

I made my voice sound hopeless. "Yeah, g'night."

"Are you okay?"

"I think so," I replied and then reached out for a tree branch to steady myself as if I'd suddenly been struck with vertigo.

"Are you sure?"

She looked tired. I had to act quickly.

"I'm fine, really," I said, steadying my grip on the tree branch.

"What's the matter? Do you feel dizzy?"

"I guess a little, but I'm fine."

"You shouldn't drive if you're dizzy."

"No, I'm fine," I said, letting go of the branch, then immediately rubbing my temples.

"No, you are not fine. You are going to sleep at my house tonight."

I'd been waiting for the chance to sleep at her house for months. And now that I'd conned her into letting me, I was light-headed from excitement. I'd been in her house a million times, but when I entered this time it felt different. The couch in the middle of the room seemed distorted, like the beginning of an acid trip, when the pillow cushions look extra poofy, but before the couch talks.

I waited in the living room while Irene changed into a pair of sweats.

"Do you want anything to sleep in?" she asked matter-of-factly, leading me to her bedroom.

It was clear our hanging-out time was over when she grabbed an extra pillow out of the closet and turned to go back to the living room.

"I don't want to take your bed," I said.

"Get a good night's sleep in the bed, since you're not feeling well," she said, closing the bedroom door behind her.

It took me a second to remember that I'd faked a major illness and that was the reason she'd invited me to sleep at her house.

"It might be meningitis," I wanted to yell back, or "I need a kidney transplant. Help."

Various other lines ran though my mind as I heard her move down the hall to the living room.

Irene irons her sheets. Everyone teases her about that. Of course, I couldn't fall asleep in her bed. I inhaled the sheets, looking for her scent. This is the bed I'll sleep in when we live together. On the back of the bedroom door hung her red, faded housedress. I sat up in bed, then walked across the room and stood at the door listening to Irene shut a kitchen cupboard. My heart pounded. I stood there listening, until the small strip of light underneath the door vanished. Then I moved face-first into her housedress, burying my nose in the soft, frayed cotton. I breathed in the place where the housedress would lie against her neck. I could smell her in the fabric.

Suddenly, I was overcome with fear that she would come back into the room for something and catch me sniffing her housedress. Or worse, she'd open the door square into my face and break my nose. Then I imagined Hope from *Days of Our Lives* tending to my broken nose. The thought of being caught sniffing Irene's housedress made me hurry back under the covers.

The sheets felt so good against my body. I couldn't believe that after so many months of pressing my nose into Irene's chest and feigning nausea, I was sleeping in her bed. For a moment it felt victorious, even though she was sleeping on the couch in the other room. I was slowly infiltrating her life like a termite boring its way into the beams in the roof. I wanted to smell every piece of clothing in her drawer. I smelled her pillow to see if it smelled like her scalp. I pushed my socks off one at a time, with the toes of the opposing foot. Then I took off my sweat pants. I was lying under her sheets with only my underwear on. My heart pounded wildly. She'd have to come in and get something in the middle of the night and I'd be ready, waiting for her.

Morning came and I'd barely slept. Every time I dozed off, I dreamed that Irene was Sinead O'Connor carrying me through the ocean naked. An expanse of light was around us. We were God's

Children enveloped in His light, except not in a religious way. I woke to the sound of Irene rummaging around the kitchen. I quickly pushed the blanket off my back, so it only covered my ass, trying to imitate Hope from *Days of Our Lives* in the Honeymoon Episode. I arched my spine so when Irene opened the door, she would see the elegant neck tendons and sinewy back muscles.

In the Honeymoon Episode, Hope had this white sheet crumpled up, barely covering her ass, and as the camera panned across her flawless back you could see the sides of her tits. I remember standing there in front of the TV with a frozen burrito in my hand, stunned and mouth wide open. Never in my life had I seen anything so fucking beautiful.

I posed in bed for two and a half hours like that, waiting for Irene to open the door and find me. The angle of my sexily craned neck, unfortunately fixed my eyes directly on the alarm clock.

6:43 A.M.

6:47 A.M.

6:49 A.M.

Where the fuck is she?

6:52 A.M.

She has to go to work.

6:52 A.M.

She's going to have to come get clothes to teach in.

6:53 A.M.

Her footsteps.

I imagined her staring at my naked back. How could I pretend to be sleeping when my heart was pounding?

6:54 A.M.

The bathroom door shut and the shower turned on.

Fuck!

I was determined to lie there all day if I had to. This might be the only time I'd ever get to sleep at her house and I wasn't going to blow it. Eventually, she'd have to come in.

6:58 A.M.

The shower turned off. She doesn't take very long showers.

I heard the bedroom doorknob turn.

She called my name. Not sweetly.

I pretended to sleep.

She said my name again.

Climb on top of me, climb on top of me.

"Time to get up, Francie. I have to leave for work in twenty minutes."

The door closed behind her.

6:59 A.M.

I got up, dumbfounded at my ineptness, and followed Irene into the kitchen to eat some multigrain gruel for breakfast.

11

IRENE IS REALLY the smartest, most amazing person I've ever met. Gustavo and Jenny didn't take The Philosophy of Nonviolence, but they were in Irene's other classes. They knew her when she was married. Gustavo showed up in Irene's office one day and gave her a letter he'd written, confessing his love to her. Irene told Gustavo it was her policy never to date her students—besides, she was married. So Gustavo dropped out of her class, and Irene separated from her husband and that was the beginning of my enormous heartbreak.

I tried to be tough with Irene. When I was in her Philosophy of Nonviolence class, I used to write really tough things in our mandatory journal. I told Irene I was in AA right away, but not nonchalantly.

"I think that was right after I got dragged to the mental hospital," I'd say just loud enough so she could hear.

"You got dragged to a mental hospital?" Irene said on cue.

"Yeah. It wasn't really a big deal."

For my final project in the Philosophy of Nonviolence class I created my own dance called the Nonviolent Shuffle. I stood completely still, not dancing. Get it? Irene laughed so hard. She gave me an A+. She's so fucking gorgeous when she laughs and when she shaved her head she became even more fucking beautiful.

Some groups of nonviolent people wear masks over their mouths and noses so they don't kill the little amoebas that float in the air. It's called Jainism. Other people don't step on the grass because they don't want to kill it. I want to be a really good person, too, but stepping on the grass seems inevitable. There was a lot of grass at the community college where Irene used to be a teacher. All of Irene's students wanted to hang out with her, but only a select few got to go to Denny's after class and talk about Jainism.

Jenny and Gustavo have been inseparable best friends since high school. They moved to San Francisco about six months before Irene did. Gustavo transferred to San Francisco State University to study philosophy and political science, but Jenny wanted a break from college, so she just got a job at a café called Muffins Muffins. Jenny and Gustavo went up to find an apartment that would later become Simplicity House, while Irene finished her teaching contract at the community college.

When Irene taught at our community college, I'd walk up and down the corridor past her classroom, hoping at some point she'd open her door, look out, and see me. On warm days when her door was open, my heart would race, the closer I got to stepping into that small diameter of open doorway. I would never look into her classroom; instead, I acted indifferent, puffing my cigarette.

Let me tell you how Irene used to dress. She wore black jeans, a black T-shirt, and black clogs. Her keys jangled from a key ring on her belt loop. She has the most beautiful cheekbones and big doe eyes. Oh my god. And her hands, her strong hands. German Expressionist hands. Huge knuckles and crooked fingers. *Peasant hands,* she calls them.

I'd drive by her house at night even though it was twenty-five minutes from where I lived, just to see if Divot's light was on. Oh, that's what we used to call Irene before we called her Chops or

Choppy. She got named Divot the night a group from the Philosophy of Nonviolence class went miniature golfing. Irene put her ball down and it rolled off the plastic where you're supposed to tee off. She said, "The ball rolled out of the divot."

"What did you call it?" I said.

"The divot, that's the name for that hole."

That was the night my love metastasized. Holy shit. She's the smartest, most intelligent woman in the whole world. She knows the name for that little thing at miniature golf.

A few holes later I said, "Can I call you Divot?"

Then everyone started calling her Divot, which kind of pissed me off, when I was the one who had thought of it.

Before Irene joined Jenny and Gustavo in San Francisco, we used to do stuff together every day. Just the two of us. Whenever we'd hang out, she'd talk about how brilliant Gustavo was but how his intensity scared her sometimes. How he has a lot of rage because he grew up in a really abusive household. Then she'd talk about how sweet and patient Jenny was and how she'd taken care of Gustavo all through high school and protected him from his crazy family. I was so happy to be hanging out with Irene, I didn't think too much about her relationship with Jenny and Gustavo. Plus, they hardly seemed real because they were so far away in San Francisco. My sole mission was to try and make Irene fall in love with me before she moved to San Francisco to be with Jenny and Gustavo. The trick was, how would I do it without letting her know I was in love with her?

Now that I'm in San Francisco I pretend like I don't love Irene anymore. I pretended like I didn't love her before, too, but since I moved to San Francisco I don't openly worship her. I know she'd never pick me over Gustavo. Even though Jenny is her lover, too, I don't feel jealous of Jenny. I guess because I know Irene doesn't love Jenny with the intensity with which she loves Gustavo.

You probably think I only speak in perpetual non sequiturs.

That's a word this sexy waitress who wears leather suspenders taught me. She doesn't work at IHOP—which is why she can wear leather suspenders when she waitresses. Her name is Polly and she works at Sparky's, the diner across town that William and I go to sometimes after our IHOP shift on Friday nights. Polly also taught me *megalomania*. *Megalomania* means a mental disorder characterized by delusions of grandeur, wealth, power, etc., a passion for doing big things, a tendency to exaggerate. I love the dictionary. For instance, I looked up *megalomania* when I got home from Sparky's that night and I read the definition for the word above it, too. *Megalocardia*—abnormal enlargement of the heart. I have that, too. That's why I love four women:

Irene

Hope from *Days of Our Lives*

Maria

Polly.

12

I WOULD RATHER be a mediocre pancake waitress than have a doctorate in mineral geology any day. Not that I think rocks and stuff are dumb. It just seems like they've been here for millions of years, so why start looking at their little stripes now? I really don't know if the Earth is closer to a thousand or a million years old. As if the number of years the Earth has been around matters. This book is about much more important things. I'm writing because I'm basically suicidal and lonely and I moved to San Francisco and I'm trying not to kill myself or drink. Or slit my arms up with razors. I'm going to try and write as much as I can by Friday, because that's when I start therapy and if I get well too quickly I may not be able to finish this. Not like getting well is a possibility. Today I was in the elevator coming up to the sixth floor and I was thinking, "What a miserable day." And then I thought, "What a miserable decade, and I'm only twenty."

* * *

I work Friday nights at IHOP. It's usually okay money. Most of the time we walk out with sixty dollars. The only annoying thing about

Friday nights is, every Friday without fail, the Pyramid People show up ten minutes before my shift is over. Then I have to stay and wait on them. They never order food. They get a plate of fries and share it between all sixteen of them or they order a hot tea and one ice-cream sundae. They're just using IHOP as a place to have their business conference. They sell a lot of useless shit: rose-shaped soap, tins of caramel covered popcorn, and wind chimes made out of recycled soda cans. They sell the same stuff that kids in junior high school sell door to door in order to keep the soccer team from going bankrupt. Not only do the Pyramid People sell their wares, they try to recruit other people to sell things, too. The ringleader once showed me a drawing of pyramids.

"See, if you're up here at the top of the pyramid," he explained, tapping the drawing with his dirty fingernail, "then you get a portion of all sales of these people under you, as well as your own commissions for the number of people you recruit. And of course you get the profit from your own sales."

This explanation was a result of me hostilely asking them, after the third consecutive week they'd come in, what their deal was. I learned everything I never wanted to know about the "Pyramid Method" in about thirty seconds.

"Your profitability has the ability to really snowball," the ringleader continued. He called himself Greg Roberts. I purposely set down his chamomile tea slightly out of his reach.

"You should consider trying it, Francesca. It's a good way to make extra cash."

"I'm not interested in selling anything," I said to him. "My mom and dad are both salespeople. It's not for me."

"Well, I bet you'd be great at it." Greg Roberts smiled.

"I don't think so."

It never ceases to amaze me, people who boast riches and success but eat at IHOP on a regular basis. I hate the pompous Pyramid People. I hate them for coming in every Friday night exactly as I'm leaving, and I hate that they order time-consuming items from the menu, like tea and ice-cream sundaes. I hate them for lingering for hours and then leaving a lousy tip. Some of the people in the group don't even order anything at all. "No, thank you," they say when I hand them a menu in a restaurant.

"What do you mean, 'No, thank you?'" I want to scream. "You're in a fucking restaurant, order something or leave."

I always have the nonsmoking section on Friday nights and they're nonsmokers, so that means inevitably they're in my section.

When I see Greg Roberts walk up to the hostess stand I say, "Goddammit!"

"Hi, Francie." He waves.

Or sometimes he says, "We're back! Did you miss us?" Then he wanders over and asks me if I've given any more thought to joining their team.

When new recruits come in, Greg Roberts says to them, "This is Francie. She's our fan-tas-tic waitress who I've been trying to convince to come on board."

"Really?" the new recruit says, "You should do it. It's great money!"

"I don't like forcing people to buy things," I mutter.

The first time Greg Roberts asked me to "come on board," I made the mistake of saying, "Uh, maybe," because I don't know how to say no to people.

"Write down your phone number and I'll give you a call this week and fill you in on what we're all about."

"Sure, okay," I said because I was trying to get out the door of IHOP and William was waiting for me in his truck.

One day when I was sleeping, the phone rang and I picked it up excitedly, thinking it might be Irene.

"Hello?"

"Francie, Greg Roberts here from the Pyramid Method."

It took me a second to realize who it was.

"Oh, hi," I said.

"Thought about coming on board yet?"

"Uh, I don't think so," I said, walking to the bathroom to get a razor blade.

"Well, let me explain a few things to you about how we work . . ."

For the next thirty minutes Greg Roberts babbled on and I carved sad faces into my ankles with the tip of the razor.

Finally after I'd even stopped responding with indifferent *uh-huhs* he said, "Well, I'll bring you some new literature about our company when I see you at IHOP."

I was so relieved when I hung up the phone, I decided to start a new carving on my other ankle while I dialed Irene.

"Hi, Goaty. What are you doing?" she asked cheerfully.

"Carving a happy face into my ankle. Wanna hang out?"

13

TONIGHT WAS THE first night Irene and I had hung out alone since I moved to San Francisco. She was wearing her thick black sweater with the little moth hole on the shoulder that I like a lot. We went to the Castro, which is the queer part of town. The street was bustling with gay men holding hands and a few surly lesbians walking their dogs. I felt exhilarated and afraid to be among so many gay people. At the same time I was a little disappointed—I'd dreamed about being in a place like the Castro for so long and I didn't feel any more at home among the gay T-shirt and condom stores than I had growing up. "Is this it?"

The entire time I carefully walked about an arm's length away from Irene. I don't want to seem desperate for her anymore, now that the cards are on the table and she knows I moved to San Francisco because I wanted to be with her. But after hours of acting aloof, I gave in to Irene's attempts to put her arm around me and walk down the street. When she taught at the community college she'd always cuddled or put her arms around her favorite students. It didn't mean anything sexual, but now for the first time in my life, I was walking with my arm around another woman in San Francisco,

surrounded by gays and T-shirt stores that supported gays. I tried
not to think about Gustavo waiting for Irene at home. There would
be some kind of drama. Had he written his paper for school or not?
Had he? Irene would be sure that he had. And then there'd be loads
and loads of psychological analyses about Gustavo, and explanations
about what it was that made him so freaked out to write a paper.
Fear of failure. Fear of success. Irene likes to steer the confused back
on track, to shepherd, mother, tend. I love and hate that about her.

After an ice-cream cone, we wound our way back to the bus stop
and waited for a bus home. I pulled my pack of cigarettes out of the
breast pocket of my motorcycle jacket and shook one out. There
were only a few left and I'd only bought the pack at noon. Normally,
I try not to smoke more than a pack a day, but when I am with Irene
I always smoke more. I lit the cigarette and sat down on the bus stop
bench. The bench was actually a small plastic seat that remained in
an upright position, until you sat down, and then it rotated into a
place to sit. Irene told me that the mayor recently had all the benches
in the bus stops changed so homeless people wouldn't be able to
sleep on them at night. I imagined a homeless person coming up to
a bus shelter after a whole day of pushing a shopping cart around
and then trying to sleep somewhere for the night and having
nothing but pieces of plastic that would lop them right on the
ground if their feet weren't placed exactly right.

"People don't believe in community, Goat," Irene started. "It's up
to us to take care of others who are less fortunate than us."

I nodded. I didn't want to hear Irene talk about everything that
needed to be done to make the world fairer. It was another reminder
of how inadequate I was, and the huge gap of social consciousness
between us. I feel like I'm a bad person when Irene and Gustavo stay
up burning candles and meditating on the eve of a child rapist's exe-
cution and I fall deep into a narcoleptic slumber, unable to hold my
candle in the vigil line. The next day, I walk next to a tired-faced
Irene and when she solemnly states the first, middle, and last name

of the executed prisoner, I all but apologize, as if I'd been the one who went around raping children or enforcing the death penalty. I felt depressed thinking about all the troubles in the world I could do nothing about.

My toes felt cold inside my boots. It was a typical cold San Francisco night. I leaned forward to see if the bus was coming and felt the breeze against my ears. Irene stood next to the bus map inside the shelter. The light shone on her stubbled head and high, strong cheekbones. I tried to memorize each line of her face, in case we were ever stripped from each other and I needed to sculpt it.

14

IRENE AND I went to the piercing place today because she's wanted to get her nose pierced for the longest time but hasn't because she felt like she was already pushing her luck at the college by having a shaved head.

"They can't fire you for getting a nose ring. Anyway, you can take it out when you go back to work."

A really tattooed girl who had her face all pierced came out from behind the curtain and asked us if we needed help.

"I'm thinking about getting my nose pierced," Irene said.

The piercer showed Irene a chart of all the different places she could get her nose pierced.

"Do you want it through your septum," the girl asked, "or through the side of the nostril?"

The septum is the middle of the nose, like what a bull looks like with a ring through its nose.

"Get it through the septum," I said.

"No, I don't think so. It's too much."

The piercer, who had her septum pierced, stared silently at Irene.

"Maybe I should get pierced, too," I said, trying to divert the piercer's attention from Irene's last comment.

The piercer told Irene, "You need to pick out a stud that you want to be pierced with."

"Can I get a hoop?" Irene asked.

"No. You can put in a hoop after six weeks. You need a stud at first if you want it to heal right."

While Irene bent over the counter looking at the jewelry. I noticed a chart of line drawings. Diagrammed faces with hoops and studs through eyebrows, noses, lips, cheeks, necks, nipples, belly buttons. Then there were genital piercings. A man had a hoop through the end of his penis and under his balls. A woman had her clit and labia pierced. There was a photo album, too, of past customers. One woman had eight or nine rings on each side of her labia, and then she had a silver lock clipping both sets of rings together. I was enthralled that people could be so brave.

"What I really want is that silver hoop," Irene said.

"If you don't care if it gets infected, you can use the hoop," the piercer said, clearly annoyed.

Irene selected an amethyst stud and the piercer led us back through a curtain.

"Should I come back, too? I don't want to be in your way," I told the piercer.

"You won't be in my way."

"Can I take this album back here?"

"Sure."

She set up her little area, pulling a sterilized needle out of a bottle, and I continued to leaf through the photo album.

"Maybe I'll get my labia pierced," I said to Irene.

I opened the page to the mutilated labia with the locket connecting all 12,000 silver rings and held it open for Irene. The piercer looked over Irene's shoulder at the book.

"Do you want your outer or inner labia pierced?" the piercer asked.

What was the difference? I'd never even heard the word *labia* until I came into the piercing store. I thought quickly about my anatomy and concluded the outer labia were too thick and would hurt too much.

"The inner, I think," I answered.

Irene looked at me. "Are you really going to get your labia pierced?"

I wanted Irene to think I was brave. Who puts a ring through their labia? No one but a crazy person.

"Why not?" I said.

The piercer told Irene to turn her head toward the bright light so she could see better.

"Is it going to hurt?" Irene asked.

"It's just a quick pinch."

Then the piercer put the gun up to Irene's nose and stuck the needle through. Irene flinched. The piercer inserted the amethyst stud and told Irene how to clean and take care of her new piercing.

"Do you want to get your labia pierced today?" the piercer asked, turning to me.

It felt like a dare. The piercer was tough—body covered in tattoos and a face full of metal. Irene's shaved head and tiny amethyst stud looked childlike by comparison. Was I tough enough to go through with it?

"Sure," I answered.

"You'll need to take your pants off," the piercer said, sounding bored.

"How much will it cost?" I asked, looking for a last-minute out.

"It's forty dollars for the piercing, plus the jewelry. If you just want a stainless steel hoop like this," she said flicking the hoop in her septum, "it's another forty dollars."

"I can lend you the money," Irene chimed in.

"Okay," I said, completely stunned at the thought of eighty dollars being spent on a ring through my labia.

"Wow, I can't believe you're going to do it," Irene said, clearly impressed.

"I'll get everything ready while you take off your pants," the piercer said.

It dawned on me suddenly that Irene wasn't going to leave the room and I'd be sitting there naked in front of her. This wasn't how I pictured her seeing me with my clothes off and I felt a slight panic, thinking that maybe the whole piercing thing was a mistake. But it was too late. The piercer was about to start. I hoped my pussy wasn't filthy.

"Are you ready?" she asked.

I simply nodded. I couldn't believe a woman was finally going to touch my pussy, even if just to pierce it. The piercer handed me a sterilizing wet nap and told me to wipe my labia off, and I did. I could feel my cheeks burning from embarrassment. Thank god Irene was standing behind me, so I couldn't tell if she was looking at me.

"So about where do you want the piercing?" the piercer asked.

"Umm, the middle's fine," I said, trying to sound unfazed.

It happened quickly, a pinch and then a burn that started at my labia and radiated throughout my body.

"I'm going to take the needle out and put the ring in here, so just sit tight a minute."

She maneuvered the ring through the hole.

"This ball snaps off and on to keep the hoop closed," the piercer said. "You just want to twist the ring around a few times a day when you shower and before bed, and clean it out to make sure it doesn't get infected, okay?"

"Okay," I said.

I slipped my underwear on carefully, and then my pants, feeling thrilled about my new, tough labia ring.

Irene paid for both of us and we left.

"I can't believe you just got your labia pierced on a whim," she said.

"That's the kind of a girl I am," I said, lighting a cigarette.

"I'm impressed," Irene said, smiling. "What do you want to do now?"

"I should probably go home and get ready for work."

"I thought you had to work at five o'clock."

"I do, but I want to take a shower and wash my IHOP dress, and then it's going to take me an hour to walk there because I don't want to spend another dollar for the bus today. Let's catch the twenty-two."

"What do you think about my nose ring?"

"It looks good. I think it's going to look really good when you can put the hoop in."

"But do I look different? Does my face look totally different?"

I looked at her face—at the beautiful crow's-feet near her eyes and the tiny patches of gray in the soft stubble on her head. And then I stared at her nose. It seemed like the same nose. Except now it had an amethyst stud in one nostril.

When we got on the bus, I slid into a window seat and Irene threw her arm around me. I felt afraid to have her arm around me on the bus. Jenny told me a story about these boys on the 22 bus that had stun guns. They snuck up behind people they thought were gay and stunned them. *I wished they'd stunned Gustavo.* When Irene taught at the community college I let her put her arms around me anywhere—even though we lived in the most homophobic town in the world—and every time she did, I melted. Now in San Francisco, surrounded by gay people, I was scared. But I didn't ask her to move her arm because I didn't want her to know I was afraid.

The bus came off the electric wires that powered it and everyone on the bus let out a collective groan. The bus driver got out and tried to hook the bus back up to the wires. Two stops later I got off to transfer to the 38. I waved good-bye to Irene, who was touching the amethyst stud inside the frame of the bus window.

At home I took a bath and turned the ring in my labia to make sure I got all the pus and crust off. The piercer said it would be crusty for a few days. Then I avoided the laundry and went to work in my dirty dress again. The whole time I was walking to work, I felt the sting of the piercing between my legs—a dull aching, and it made me excited that I had this thing—this ring in me that nobody knew about if they just looked at me.

15

I HAD A death wish growing up. It's a miracle I'm alive, really. I drank hairspray and tried to suck the ink out of ballpoint pens. Once at a party I sprayed Windex into my mouth as a party trick. Classmates brought me pills from their parents' medicine chests and I'd take whatever they gave me without even asking what it was. Once my friend Wendy gave me some of her father's blood pressure pills during wood shop and I broke out into such a rash I had to go to the nurse.

"I've never seen anything like this," the nurse said, sending me home for the day.

In science class, after we burned something on the Bunsen burner for an experiment, some arrogant honors kid would slide the ashy substance over to me to snort. In exchange, they'd let me cheat off them on tests. I was like a sideshow for the university-bound students.

The first time I really tried to kill myself was in the middle of my tenth-grade English class. I can't remember why I even decided to, but the next thing I knew I had taken the hall pass during a Shakespeare lecture and found myself at the drinking fountain swallowing thirty-two Tylenol tablets, one at a time, with thirty-two sips of water. Would you believe me if I told you I never told anyone? I should've had my stomach pumped, but instead I got a terrible headache and went and watched my brother's soccer game. Everything smelled like Tylenol for days.

The second time I really wanted to kill myself was two years ago. I'd been creeping toward admitting I was gay, reading classified ads for gay and lesbian support groups and sneaking into Hollywood to go to the one lesbian coffee shop and the gay bookstore. My heart almost beat out of my chest just walking into that bookstore. I cut out WOMEN SEEKING WOMEN personal ads from the back of the *LA Weekly* and carried them around in my pocket, trying the phone numbers from pay phones only to realize the voicemail boxes couldn't be accessed by pay phone.

Outside the public library had become my new hideout. There I'd write Irene letters, telling her how I felt once and for all, while smoking seven thousand cigarettes and listening to the same Violent Femmes cassette. After a number of attempts to word my love for her just right, I'd crumple up the letters and throw them into the giant blue trash can in front of the library.

The few gay books in the library were dismal: a Martina Navratilova biography, and *Go Ask Alice* versions of gay runaways. I hid in a tiny study cubicle and secretly read the true accounts of young gays who were kicked out of their houses and had to turn to street hustling and gas huffing. It was nighttime when I'd leave the library. My head hurt from concentrating on the bleak stories. I drove my tiny red hatchback to the next town where I lived. One night I stopped at a red light and it hit me that I was gay and there was no getting out of it. I didn't just love Irene. I was part of a whole class of people that the world hated. The adrenaline I'd accumulated from sneaking around the library reading about "gay" people evaporated and I was filled with despair. I was gay.

My only choice was to kill myself. I already knew one guy who'd killed himself because he was gay. He was eighteen and fed a garden hose from the exhaust pipe of his car through the driver's window, filling the car with carbon monoxide.

How would I do it? I felt a calmness take over me that comes out of every option disappearing. I'll drive into a wall. No. I'll take a bottle of pills.

The light changed and Sid Vicious came on the radio singing "I Wanna Be Your Dog." I turned up the volume. I wanted to be Irene's dog. I decided temporarily to not kill myself. I'd run away to San Francisco and try to make Irene fall in love with me. If I couldn't, then I'd reconsider suicide or maybe I'd try to seduce someone beautiful like Hope from *Days of Our Lives*.

16

APPARENTLY GOD'S PLAN for me was to ring in the New Year as a five-dollar-an-hour IHOP hostess. It's hard to describe IHOP on New Year's Eve.

Julio called me at six that evening and said, "I need you to hostess tonight. It's an emergency."

I didn't have anything better to do. Maria had a date with Ashanti, and Irene, Jenny, and Gustavo were going to a gospel concert at their church. It's the kind of church where everyone has to turn around and hug their neighbor at some point in the program. Julio wanted me to work from nine at night until six the next morning. And unless some cute lesbian came in and fucked me in the bathroom before midnight, I was going to ring up another year as a big V virgin. "Hey, look everybody—it's the big V. I wonder why she can't get any ass wearing that IHOP dress."

The first three and a half hours passed quietly, affirming my belief that even the freaks don't want to celebrate New Year's Eve at IHOP unless they happen upon it in the middle of an unexpected PCP binge.

I tried to keep myself busy, continually cleaning the glass on the dessert carousel. The dessert carousel has four levels, filled with the kinds of desserts found in coloring books—flamboyant chocolate cakes, tricolored glass goblets of Jell-O with perfect puffs of whipped cream on top, four-inch-thick carrot and coconut cake, chocolate pudding—all of it swirls around the entire day, immediately in front of where I stand behind the cash register.

There's a clock on the wall behind the dessert carousel. In order to see the clock, you have to look through the gap between the tall goblets of Jell-O and the rice pudding as they spin past.

"What time is it?" someone asks.

I lower my head and wait for the gap between desserts. It took me a month of slow Thursday night dinner shifts to get good at telling time through the dessert carousel.

When a customer comes to the hostess stand with a big attitude and asks me what time it is, I say, "Hang on just a minute," then I hunch down. "I just have to wait until the Jell-O goes by so I can see the clock."

Because New Year's Eve was supposed to be so busy, the hostess tasks were divided. My task was to keep the waiting list. Enrique, the senior host, was to ring up people, and Roxanne was going to seat customers.

Enrique is barely five feet tall, with thick black curly hair to his shoulders and unusually soft hands. The cooks call him faggot because he paints his nails with clear polish and likes to sneak up behind other workers and squeeze their hands when they aren't looking. It doesn't matter if you're a guy or a girl.

"His hands are soft like a breast, it's really weird," that's what William told me when I first started. I assumed William was just like all the other straight guys and didn't like Enrique because he seemed gay. But then one day, Enrique grabbed my hand and squeezed it, and his hand did feel boneless, soft and breast-like.

As he stood before me, I was caught between two thoughts. One was, "Please don't grab my hand," and the other one was, "Oh god, I want to feel a woman's breast."

I like working with him, because we hide behind the telephone when it's slow and stare at the space below the heat lamp, waiting for a mistake that we can scoop up and take into the bathroom to eat. Whenever I hostess, I always forget to put money in my dress pocket for an employee meal, and New Year's Eve was no different.

"Enrique, I'm so hungry."

"Me, too, baby."

"What time is it?" Enrique asked.

"It's eleven-thirty," I said, looking through the dessert carousel.

"This fucking sucks," Roxanne groaned.

Roxanne spends most of her free time upstairs, chain-smoking and snorting speed. She always makes me think of my mother because her car is exactly the make and year of my mother's car, except a darker brown, and the ashtray is stale and overflowing. When she gives me a ride home it makes me feel like I am fifteen again, driving somewhere with my mother.

Roxanne is a goth speed freak and her arms are lined with pink marks. At first I thought she cut herself with razors, but when I asked her, she said her asshole boyfriend used to throw darts at her from his recliner when he got drunk. Her story is that each pink mark represents a place where a dart hit her.

"You should leave him if he throws darts at you," I said, offering what little relationship advice I could.

"I can't afford to move out right now," she replied, "and anyway it doesn't really matter, because I have a new boyfriend he doesn't know about."

Roxanne's dress is always dirty and wrinkled like mine. She wears thick black eyeliner, and pencils her eyebrows into giant arches. Julio usually makes her go into the bathroom and wash most of her eyebrows off, but on New Year's he ignored them because he knew it was going to be busy and he'd need her. I stared at the lumpy parts of Roxanne's hair, where she'd rushed to put it into a ponytail without combing it, and wondered if my hair looked as bad.

Julio came out of his office with a bag of party favors and handed out horns, rattles, and silver-paper top hats to all of us as if they were our regulated medication.

"At midnight," Julio said, "I want you guys to run through the restaurant blowing these horns, Okay? Let's wish everyone a Happy New Year."

Tim rolled his eyes after Julio walked away. He was already pissed about having to work on what he said might be the last New Year's Eve of his life.

"Julio can go fuck himself, if he thinks I'm going to run through this restaurant in an aluminum foil top hat and blow a goddamned paper horn at midnight," Tim fumed.

His eyes started to do the giant bug thing they do when he gets upset. I didn't want to run through the restaurant either, but it seemed like the rare, valid, opportunity to release aggressions while wearing my IHOP dress.

The restaurant was less than half full when Julio began the midnight countdown.

"Ten, nine, eight, seven, six, five, four, three, two, one . . ."

Julio leaned over my shoulder and whispered, "Go on."

His hand nudged me between my shoulders and I began to jog through the restaurant, my nurse shoes squeaking.

"WAAAH, HAPPY NEW YEAR! WAAAHH! WOO-HOO, HAPPY NEW YEAR," I screamed at a terrified old man, bent over his chicken-fried steak.

It was a vicious cycle. Yelling made the humiliation feel manageable, yet the more I yelled the more humiliated I felt. I thought I'd keep doing it, and pretend like I didn't care. "HAPPY NEW YEAR, HAPPY NEW YEAR EVERYONE AT FABULOUS IHOP, WOO-HOO, YEAH, ALL RIGHT."

I looked at Julio for approval, putting both my thumbs up in mock excitement.

"Okay, okay, settle down," Julio told me. "Let's put the horn away and get back to work."

None of the other employees had done anything but blow their horns dutifully and hide next to the salad bar. I saw Tim dig into his apron for what I was sure was a Valium.

As the night wore on, Julio had proven himself right. The restaurant filled up with people. They started to file in around twelve-thirty, all dressed up. There were several women wearing the zebra-striped coat that I had walked past every day for the last month in the window of Dottie's Dress Up. The store tries to appeal to the tigress within everyone.

"Nothing over $19.99," the sign promises.

A lot of drag queens shop there. Drunken ladies in zebra coats leaned toward me, asking how long until a table would be available.

"How long, how long?"

Where was Irene? She said she'd stop by and I wanted to look good. It was so hard to look good in the IHOP dress. As time passed and no new tables opened up, the crowd started to panic. A few customers even tried to bribe me IHOP-style, by folding a dollar up twenty times and slipping it to me. People who are lousy tippers use this same technique. They fold one dollar into a million little folds so it seems like it's more than one dollar when they sneak it into your palm.

"See what you can do for us. Okay, baby?" one idiot crooned.

I waved him away, telling him in the loudest and most chastising voice I could that everybody had to wait their turn. "It wouldn't be fair if just because you gave me a single dollar, that I put you before these other people who have waited almost an hour, would it?"

Usually this technique worked—but the idiot came back a second time with the same folded dollar that he didn't even try to conceal. He teetered back and forth, holding the dollar in my face. He looked like he might fall over.

"If that was a hundred-dollar bill, then we could talk," I told him.

"I got a hundred-dollar bill, baby," he slurred.

He reeked of cologne and peppermint schnapps. I know the smell of peppermint schnapps well, since I drank it every day for an entire semester in high school. The cologne smelled toxic, like burning brakes.

"Where's my name on the list?" he asked.

"Exactly where it was the last time you checked, five minutes ago."

"Thanks, sexy," he said sarcastically, holding the dollar up in front of me, to let me know I'd lost my chance to have it, before he put it in his pocket.

Around three o'clock in the morning I saw Irene, Jenny, and Gustavo trying to fight their way through the crowd of waiting people. Irene caught my eye through the glass and gave a big maternal wave. I tried to make myself look pathetic, hoping she'd come hug me. Then I realized I looked pathetic anyway. She gave me a big, loving hug, the kind you give to someone after an earthquake has wiped out their family. Gustavo stood passively at her side in his tie and dress shoes.

"Got the dress shoes on, huh?" I said to him.

"Yep. How's your New Year going?" he asked, trying to sound sweet.

I gave him the "I hate everyone" look.

"Well, we just wanted to stop by and say Happy New Year," Irene said. "We can't stay and you look busy."

That's right, go fuck your ten-years-younger boyfriend.

Jenny must have seen the pained look in my face because she, too, gave me a big hug. "Goaty, I'm sorry you have to spend your New Year's working at IHOP."

Her hair smelled clean, and I didn't want to pull away from her. I love when she calls me Goaty. I wished I could leave and go sleep on the blue mattress on Jenny's floor. We could cuddle and eat cookies like we used to do when I first moved here, and tell jokes and hug, and not think about Irene and Gustavo in the next room. Why couldn't I have fallen in love with Jenny? She's so nice and she hates ratatouille, too.

By 5 A.M. the restaurant had thinned out a bit. Julio told me to clean the women's bathroom, which was trashed. There were paper towels all over the place and crushed-out cigarettes in the sink. The bathroom reeked of puke and I had to hold my breath to continue working. I managed to make a glove out of a paper towel, and began picking up all the trash off the floor. I caught a glimpse of myself in the bathroom. My hair was a mess and I had dark circles under my eyes. Depressed, I fished my pack of cigarettes out of my dress pocket and lit one. I couldn't have felt uglier. Suddenly, one of the stall doors flung open and a woman in a zebra coat came out, looking white as a ghost. How many of these coats existed? She stumbled past me and for a fleeting moment I had the urge to tell her that her life didn't have to be this way—she could go to AA. Instead I let her go by.

I stared at the floor in disbelief. There was no way I was going to clean up drunken people's puke for five dollars an hour. You'd have to pay me fifteen or twenty dollars an hour to do that. I started to cry. I hated everybody and the crazy surge of hopelessness I sometimes get where all of a sudden I want to step in front of a truck was taking me over. The sound of the bathroom fan turning around and around was making me feel even more anxious. Fed up, I went to find Julio.

"You can't be finished cleaning already," he said.

"There's puke everywhere! I can't take it anymore!" I said, beginning to cry.

He laughed.

"Go home, Francesca," he said. "Don't cry. Be happy. I'll see you tonight at five."

I changed into my torn gray sweatpants and T-shirt and balled my uniform up into my backpack. I'd forgotten to bring a change of shoes. I'd have to walk the whole way home in my nurse shoes.

I remembered there was a 7 A.M. AA meeting at the Dry Dock in the Marina, which was only a few blocks from IHOP. When I got there my legs tingled as I walked toward the tower of Styrofoam cups that stood next to the shiny coffee pot.

"We admitted we were powerless over alcohol, that our lives had become unmanageable," an old man read.

The room was almost filled with recovering alcoholics. One person after the next shared how they'd managed to not drink through a usually stressful holiday. I wanted to raise my hand and say something that could explain my night. My eyes felt heavy and I could smell my armpits. I wondered who else could smell them. Looking around the room, I saw another pair of nurse shoes. My heart quickened for a second, wondering if someone else from IHOP was in AA. My eyes followed the nurse shoes up to the face they belonged to. It was an old lady.

"We are fully self-supporting through our own contributions . . ." someone read, passing a basket around the room. "Contributions help pay for rent, coffee . . ."

Most people contributed a dollar to help cover the expenses. I thought of all the bus fares in that basket. I thought of the folded-dollar man, the zebra coats, nervous Julio. I thought of Irene, Gustavo, and Jenny and of Roxanne's lies about her dart-throwing boyfriend. When I got home, I flung myself on my mattress. I couldn't believe I had made it another year. It was 8 A.M. and my apartment was already pretty sunny. I'd have to remember to look at the Salvation Army for curtains if I kept working graveyard shifts.

17

TODAY IS SIXTY days sober and three days without a cigarette. Irene went down south with Gustavo to meet his family. I've been working on my poetry, going to AA, and hanging out with Jenny. It's been nice. We usually get a cup of coffee and chain-smoke, or sometimes we go to the Tumbleweed Café, which is this really cute restaurant on Van Ness Street that has pink neon pigs that blink and it looks like they're running around the windows. The Tumbleweed Café has the best hamburgers. Jenny found out about it accidentally one day when she was walking down Van Ness Street. She saw the flashing pigs and went in. I always order the Texas Burger, which is bacon, cheese, and guacamole, and we share a strawberry milkshake. God it's so good to eat there and then smoke our brains out, and talk about writing.

Jenny made a zine with some of her poems and cool quotes from Audre Lorde and Gandhi. She titled it *Puking Roses*. Most of the poems are about being in love with Irene but feeling like she can't totally have her. I guess everyone is writing unattainable love poems for Irene. I leafed through the zine until I tuned to a poem called "Tables."

When Jenny saw what page I was on, she said shyly, "That poem is for you."

The idea of someone writing a poem for me took a second to register.

"What do you mean it's for me?"

Jenny shrugged and blew cigarette smoke out the side of her mouth. Her dirty-blond hair was coming out in all directions from under her fucked-up Army hat. I stared into her blue eyes.

Under the title "Tables" was the inscription *for Goaty.*

It's a poem about hating the distance that's always between us— how we're always sitting across from each other, smoking or drinking coffee, and all she wants is to break through that distance and kiss my scars, and get lost in the tangles of my hair. I could feel her waiting for my reaction to the poem. Her words were the thing I had waited for my whole life—an impossibility coming true. It was similar to when Irene said, "Move to San Francisco, Goaty. Dance in the moonlight with me and Gustavo and Jenny. We'll live simply but well and nonviolently." Except even that wasn't perfect. It would've been perfect if she'd just said, "Move here" and nothing about dancing in the moonlight with Gustavo and Jenny. Jenny had given something just to me. The whole poem was mine and I didn't have to share it.

My heart slammed inside my chest, and I tried to play it cool even though my cheeks were burning. *She wants to kiss my scars,* she wants to get lost in the tangles of my hair. She wants to "smash all these tables where we sit across from each other smoking." I reached for a cigarette and lit it, trying not to look flustered.

We didn't talk about the poem, since we were both stricken with shyness. I just told her she was an amazing poet. Jenny gave me my own copy of *Puking Roses,* and when I got home I reread "Tables" about six times, trying to figure out what she meant by it. Was she saying let's sleep together or was it just the intense talk of poets loving each other's struggles? That would be really weird if she wanted to sleep with me. I hadn't really thought about sleeping with Jenny before now, but I was immediately filled with disappointment when I realized she'd probably no sooner commit to me than Irene. After all, most of the poems in *Puking Roses* were for Irene.

18

THE NEXT DAY when Jenny called to see if I wanted to hang out there was something in her voice—shyness or coyness—that I'd never heard before. It gave me that same excited feeling I had when I read the line in her poem that said she wanted to *kiss my scars*. Walking to Simplicity House I knew what was going to happen. I was excited, but nauseated, too. I tried to call Maria from a pay phone in front of the XXX sex shop, but she wasn't home. Everyone was gone for the holidays. Even if Maria had answered I probably wouldn't have been able to ask her what I'd wanted: *What does it mean when someone says they want to kiss your scars? Oh, Maria, how do you have sex with a woman?* But I knew what was unfolding. It was like watching someone get hit in the face with a baseball. There's no way you can stop it—the ball heading for their big, medically uninsured nose, and their arms coming up a second too late to try and cover their face. Smash. The beautiful trail of crimson blood streams down their nose onto the front of their shirt. I just knew. I knew walking to Simplicity House under the overcast sky, and I knew waiting downstairs after ringing her doorbell, and I knew hands stuffed into the pockets of my motorcycle jacket as we walked down Van Ness to the Marina. I knew on the pier when she came up behind me to put her arms around me, and when the drizzle turned into hard rain, and I stood facing the rough, black waves. I finally knew.

"Do you remember what the rain meant in *The Catcher in the Rye?*" Jenny asked.

"I can't remember," I answered, trying to light a cigarette.

"Change," she said. "Big change," she said, squeezing her arms around me tightly.

We giggled, shivering, and letting the rain pelt our faces. I was high, afraid to turn around and change the fact that I actually had a woman's arms around me in this kind of way. In the way that she came to me first, not like me forcing situations, burrowing into Irene's arms when her arms weren't around someone else. *Jenny put her arms around me. Jenny wrote a poem for me.*

When we started to really freeze from standing in the cold rain, we decided to take the bus back to Simplicity House.

"Do you know how stinky goats are when they're wet?" Jenny cackled, pushing me into the window seat on the bus.

Her eyes looked diabolical, like she'd just smoked crack.

"I wish you were a cigarette," I said shoving the top of my head impulsively into her chest, and then digging my nose into her neck. "But I guess then you wouldn't smell so good."

I bit her neck lightly and then we looked away from each other shyly. When we got off the bus it was pouring harder than ever, but we were so drenched, it didn't matter. We ran the two blocks from the bus stop to Simplicity House holding hands. At her doorstep, she dug the key into the lock and pushed open the door. We ran up the three flights of stairs, our wet shoes squeaking on the plastic-covered stairs. Simplicity House always smells funny. Like some seven-grain bread. It reminded me of Irene. I looked at her handmade sign above the sink that said, "All work is meditation."

"Maybe I should go home," I said nervously.

Jenny was putting the teapot on the stove and turned to me, startled.

"Why, Goaty?"

"I want to enter a first book contest and the deadline is in two days." We stood there saying nothing for a second, both of us knowing I was looking for an out. "Plus, I need a cigarette."

"We can smoke, Goaty. We'll just open the windows and Irene will never find out. You can go home after your clothes are dry. You'll get sick if you stay in wet clothes."

Jenny stepped closer and put her hand into the waistband of my pants, tugging me toward her.

"Let's get in bed and get warm. It's a warm, dry place for goats."

In the bedroom she tackled me onto the futon. Then she unlaced my boots and pulled them off. The teapot started to whistle in the other room. She ran into the kitchen, yelling over her shoulder, "Take your clothes off, Goaty, and I'll go put them in the dryer."

I tried to rip off my shirt and pants as fast as possible before Jenny came back and saw me naked. My feet were freezing from my dripping socks.

"I found hot chocolate, Goaty! Do you want hot chocolate?"

"I want a cigarette!"

"I'm gonna bring you hot chocolate and an ashtray!"

Everything else is a blur, really. I just remember the house was freezing and then Jenny set two cups of hot chocolate on the floor next to the futon, stripped her wet clothes off, jumped into dry ones, and gathered all the clothes into her arms. She has the skinniest legs—they're so cute. They look abnormal because she has such big breasts. I wasn't looking at them lecherously. I was just huddling under the blanket waiting for her to return from the laundry room.

When she got back, there was no discussion—I fell into her mouth, her into mine. We didn't even stop to think. My body moved around her body, my cheek rubbed across her belly, hands on her breasts. We made out forever. It was as if I was possessed, drugged, led to this moment my whole life. I couldn't get over how soft she felt, how unbelievably soft her mouth was. I sucked on her nipples and moved my hands all over her warm body. Then I went down on her. I just found myself there, kissing her thighs and nibbling on the skin. She was breathing hard, and her skin grew even hotter.

I didn't know I made her come. I didn't even know how to make her come. I just kept kissing and biting her until she had to push me off, panting, "You're going to kill me, Goaty."

Coming is such an abstract thing. In my head I compare it to coming in pornography, which isn't real coming. Everyone knows real people don't come like porn people. It's like the only definitions for coming exist in health textbooks or porn movies. So how was some dumb lesbo virgin like me supposed to know when I had made Jenny come?

If Jenny hadn't said, "I haven't come that hard in a long time," I never would've known. Immediately I got the urge to cut myself because of my lack of knowledge.

"Goaty, have you had lots of girlfriends?"

"I've fooled around a little," I lied.

"How do you know how to go down so good?"

"You just felt so good."

"You feel good, too, Goaty," Jenny said, biting down hard on my neck.

I was filled with panic at the thought of her attention being focused solely on me.

"I'm good right now," I said, sliding out from under her.

Then we held each other for a long time. My urge to cut myself subsided a little as I let her press her sweaty body against me. Was I really finally in bed with such a sweet woman who wanted to be in bed with me, too? It seemed inconceivable. I traced my finger across her collarbones and the hollow of her neck, saying nothing, hypnotized by the curves and lines of her body. At first she was joking around, calling me Hungry Goaty. Then gradually she got quieter, like something was on her mind. The room started to feel cold, and I wished the radiator would come on.

I swallowed a mouthful of the cold hot chocolate. It tasted good mixing with the saltiness of Jenny that was still on my mouth.

"What's up?" I asked Jenny. "Why are you so quiet?"

"I feel guilty about cheating on Irene."

For the first time in my fucking life I'd almost forgotten Irene existed.

"Why would she be mad?" I asked, "She's probably sleeping with Gustavo right now."

I felt a surge of anger at that thought.

"Yeah, well if we have sex with anyone outside of Simplicity House we're supposed to discuss it first."

"I didn't know."

It didn't seem fair that Jenny needed Irene's permission to sleep with me. My stomach tightened as I looked at her sad and nervous eyes. Trying to lighten the mood, I gave her neck a little nibble and said, "You're not even allowed to sleep with goats?"

"This can't happen again," Jenny said. "This has to be a one-time thing."

"That's cool," I replied, trying not to sound hurt.

"And we can't tell Irene."

"What do you mean?"

"Irene will freak out. We can't tell her."

"Jenny, I don't want to lie to Irene."

Suddenly, I felt adamant about not betraying Irene.

"Goaty, trust me. We can't tell her and we can't sleep together again."

My whole body filled with dread.

"When does Irene come back?" I asked.

"The day after tomorrow."

"So we still have a few days to figure things out, right?"

Jenny got up and went downstairs for the laundry. When she came back up she tossed the small pile of clothes on the futon. My pants were still damp, but I put them on anyway. I walked down all three flights of stairs with the cigarette in my mouth, dying to light it.

19

IF I WAS depressed and freaked out before sleeping with Jenny, I was even more so after I called to check on her. We hadn't talked since we slept together two days ago.

"I don't understand why we can't just tell Irene," I pleaded.

"Because she's been betrayed a lot in her life," Jenny said.

"I don't want to hurt her, but I really don't want to lie to her."

It never even occurred to me Irene would be jealous because she was so consumed by Gustavo. But I guess subconsciously I must've known something might happen between Jenny and me, otherwise I wouldn't have waited until Irene was out of town to have sex with Jenny. And the worst part is, all I want to do now is have sex with Jenny. I feel so guilty about that, but it's true. After all, Jenny was the one that started this whole thing by saying she wanted to kiss my scars and putting her arms around me on the pier. Whatever happens, I don't want to seem desperate and needy.

I still don't understand why Jenny slept with me. When we were in bed she said she's been attracted to me since I first moved to San Francisco and she loves that we can talk about writing, but I don't know if I believe her. I think it's more likely that she slept with me because she's going through a rough spot with Irene.

*   *   *

I didn't want to go to work tonight because I wanted to have sex with Jenny again. It's the last chance we had to be alone before Irene and Gustavo get back. I wanted to kiss her skinny little legs and bite her neck. I wanted the first time to happen all over again. If Maria were home she'd know what I should do. I wrote Jenny a poem.

> *"Jenny's Poem"*
> *You*
> *Pulled me toward you*
> *Like a heavy bag of groceries.*

*   *   *

Maria finally called me back. She said she could tell by my tone of voice that my panicked phone messages had something to do with sex. That made me feel proud for a second, like finally I had sex problems that involved having sex. For so long I've had sex problems that involved being a virgin. She said being honest with Irene is the only way, so I called Jenny again. She still didn't want to tell her, but agreed she would when Irene came home. I think she was afraid I'd tell Irene the truth if she didn't. God, I feel like such a loser for turning into the kind of person who sleeps with someone else's girl-friend. That's so fucked. As far as Irene goes, I'd be surprised if she still even wanted to be my friend.

> *"Another Poem for Jenny"*
> *Looking back as if it*
> *Were years*
> *And not three*

Days ago
I don't remember seeing
Birds or puddles
Or moisture
Clinging to the side
Of the apartment building.
I don't know really
What happened
How we could be standing at the pier
The rain was—

20

BEING HONEST WITH Irene was tougher than I thought.
What a scene. When I arrived at their place, Irene was in the bedroom crying and Gustavo was consoling her. Irene felt betrayed by
both of us but especially by Jenny. I wasn't in as much trouble as
Jenny because technically I wasn't Irene's lover, nor was I a member
of Simplicity House or beholden to any of its rules. But I think deep
down Irene was less concerned about Jenny sleeping with someone
than that being a sign that she was losing her grip over her. But it
didn't take long for Irene to get her grip back.

I wanted to kiss Jenny so badly when Irene was in the other
room. There was this moment where we were just sitting in the
kitchen in silence, listening to Irene sob and I was staring at Jenny's
lips. I reached across the table to touch them, and there was a second
where she hesitated, like she wanted me to touch them, but then she
backed her chair up from the table and stood up.

"You should probably go home, Goaty," she said, not meeting
my eyes.

Jenny curled back inside Irene's fist like a dollar bill.

Irene sought domination, which took me a while to see. Particu-
larly since she talked so much about nonviolence.

Jenny sought peace.

Gustavo sought to reenact all the bullshit of his abusive childhood.

I wanted everything: Irene's cheekbones, empathy, and wisdom—Jenny's passion and kindness—the sheer beauty and curves of Maria—and the impossibility of Hope from *Days of Our Lives*.

* * *

I was so fucked up from the drama at Simplicity House that I bought a small bottle of vodka from the liquor store next to my house. I felt like the whole thing was my fault but also I was afraid that now I was going to truly be alone. Jenny would ultimately choose Irene over me, and Irene would be too hurt by my actions to ever trust me again.

I held the vodka for a long time, feeling the bottle in my sweaty hand and thinking about twisting off the plastic top. *How far would I go? Huh? Huh?* I threatened myself in the full-length mirror on the back of my closet door. I had already drank over Irene once. Now I could drink over Jenny and Irene. But if I drank I wouldn't be able to see Maria anymore. After a few hours of threatening myself in the mirror, I realized I didn't really want to drink and decided to cut myself instead.

Later I took the vodka back to the store. I couldn't deal with wasting five dollars on the bottle and then not drinking it. The owner was completely pissed off that I was bringing it back. He sold booze to all the homeless alcoholics—I'm sure no one ever tried to return vodka.

"You can't return that. You already took it home," he said.

"It's not even open."

"I can't just take it back. You bought it. You can't buy it and then bring it back."

I wanted to take the five bucks I paid for it and drop it in the wall.

"Please. I didn't even open it."

He flung the cash register drawer open and handed me my five dollars.

"If you don't want it, don't buy it. Next time I won't give you your money back."

* * *

I haven't been to an AA meeting since I bought the bottle of vodka. I know drinking again isn't going to make Jenny call me, but I want to talk to her so badly. I know she's mad at me for insisting we tell Irene the truth. But "we" didn't tell Irene. She did. And she took the brunt of Irene's wrath for doing it.

As if all this wasn't depressing enough, today I found out Maria has MS. I can't believe it. I don't know anything about MS. Tomorrow I'll go to the library and check out as many MS books as I can so I can help Maria if she needs me. After I found out about Maria I made an offering to the Goddess like she taught me to. I wrote on a piece of paper that I would amend all my defects of character as best I could if the Goddess would prevent Maria from suffering. As part of the ritual I burned the paper. Goddess, your will not mine be done.

> *"For Maria"*
> *I wish I knew who to pray to*
> *I wish you a memory of*
> *A new body*
> *A memory of a mother*
> *Who took you into department*
> *stores and held your hand*
> *while the two of you*
> *posed as mannequins for fun.*

The other night I had a dream that I called Maria, and I wasn't drunk but I sounded like it. I kept saying, "I'm not drunk." And she said something like, "Don't waste my time. I'm not coming to get you if you're drunk."

That's the second time I've dreamed I'm pretending to be sober to Maria. Last night I had a dream and Jenny was one of the people in it. It wasn't actually her—but I knew it was her I was kissing. But she wasn't into it and she kept pulling away.

* * *

Things calmed down about a week after the blowup with Irene. At least we're all talking now. The good thing that came out of telling Irene the truth was that all the rules of Simplicity House that have to do with sex have been dissolved. Irene just asked that if anyone sleeps around they have safe sex, but from now on no one in the house is committed to anyone else sexually.

When Irene and I went to have coffee for the first time after this mess, I was so afraid she was going to tell me that she didn't want me in her life anymore. She said I hurt her by sleeping with Jenny, but she can't blame, me since it wasn't like I was in a committed relationship like Jenny was with her and Gustavo. Then Irene surprised me and said she and Gustavo are rethinking their relationship—whatever the hell it is—and trying to decide if they should remain nonsexual life partners or not. I guess Gustavo hasn't wanted to have sex with Irene in a long time. She didn't come out and say that, but that's what it sounded like.

The other night Jenny and I were in the kitchen having tea while Irene was in the living room helping Gustavo with his Kafka paper, and Jenny flirted with me for the first time since the whole nightmare confession to Irene. Her flirting felt like a dare because Irene was in the next room. I leapt on the dare, pushed Jenny against the sink, and kissed her. Then we pulled away as fast as we could because suddenly we felt guilty and afraid of getting caught. Even though we weren't "technically" breaking any rules, I didn't want to rub anything in Irene's face. But now I'm confused all over again. I think before Jenny and I go any further with things we should figure out what we're doing and maybe discuss that with Irene.

The other problem is my feelings for Maria are fairly strong. I don't know if I have a crush on her or what. But I want to be really careful to not get sucked in by it. When I met Maria I couldn't imagine anyone could be that sexy. The only time I've ever seen that level of beauty is on television. But she's also so together. She's an artist and she's sober and she doesn't throw crazy fits. Fuck—she's so out of my league. And if this attraction continues to grow I need to get a new sponsor. I'm not completely obsessed with her yet, but I easily could be. Yesterday after the AA meeting, we had such a good time getting wired on coffee and laughing. But I feel like she knows how dorky I am when it comes to women. She must see I am this socially inept totally unseductive woman. Plus, she's probably looking for someone who is really together now that she has MS. When I slit my arms up and went to Maria's in the middle of the night in the cab, she was so nice to let me sleep there, even though she was on a date. But I can't go running to her every night, just so I can sleep at her house.

21

THE GIRL IN my building with the pierced nose who has done nothing but snarl at me since the day I moved in smiled at me today. Maybe she doesn't recognize me when I'm not in my IHOP uniform. I want more than anything to put on the page exactly what I am feeling—not physically, not that I have a nicotine headache and I'm starving. There are sirens constantly going by this window. I've stopped wondering why there are so many sirens. I don't think, "shooting, drug overdose, gay bashing," or that the eighty-year-old lady in the MUNI station who plays the organ has finally died. I don't think "oh my god, oh my god what tragic thing has happened?" anymore. I just keep doing what I'm doing.

I wish this chair wasn't so annoying. I'm sitting in the torn black swivel chair without a base that I got from Jenny's boss Jill at Muffins Muffins. Try writing Muffins Muffins on a job application. Even though the chair didn't have a base, I was desperate. I carried it home on the MUNI at rush hour upside down with the black vinyl cushion seat resting on my head. What a nightmare! My neck was killing me from trying to hold up the weight of a chair made of solid metal.

On the MUNI, people gave me nasty looks because they thought I was taking up too much space, but the only way I could maneuver the chair was to rest it on top of my head. Jill said in the old days everything was made out of metal instead of plastic, that's why the chair weighs so much. Jill has the prettiest neck. She said she would've helped me carry the chair to the train but she was late meeting her boyfriend for dinner. I wonder if she saw me staring at her pretty neck and that's why she told me about her *boyfriend*. She'd let me know right now what was what, in case I was getting any ideas.

Once the chair was home, I put a folded-up piece of cardboard underneath it so the jagged metal bottom wouldn't rip the shitty carpet. When you sit in the Muffins Muffins chair, it tilts from one side to the other—which brings us back to why Jenny's boss Jill was throwing it out. The only other furniture in my apartment is the orange-and-green lawn chair.

* * *

Jenny and I decided to give up trying to be celibate with each other. Plus, Jenny said, Irene and Gustavo are probably sleeping together despite what Irene says. That was all I needed to hear to make me feel entitled to have sex with whoever I wanted.

Last night she came over so we could go to a café and work on our poems. When I opened the door to let her into my apartment she tackled me onto the mattress and quickly straddled my stomach. Her eyes had the same slightly possessed look I'd seen the first time we slept together.

"You're a bad, bad, goat."

"Why?"

"For eating so many tin cans," Jenny said, pulling up the bottom of my T-shirt and kissing my stomach.

"Maybe we should think about this," I stalled half-heartedly. If I'd learned anything in my first weeks of having sex it was the power of playing hard to get.

"Okay," she mocked, pinning my arms down.

The heat of her pussy pressed into my stomach through her pants.

"Maybe we should have a cigarette first," I said.

When she leaned over to grab the pack of cigarettes, I flipped her off me and pinned down her wrists.

"Bad Goaty!" she cackled, before biting down on my forearm.

I looked at the indentation her teeth had made and grinned, before leaning forward to kiss her. Our mouths moved effortlessly over each other just as they had the first time we had sex.

"Take your shirt off," I said, trying to catch my breath. My heart pounded as I watched her pull off her shirt and bra.

"Give me a cigarette," Jenny said. She had a shy expression as she lay there shirtless.

I took a deep drag of my cigarette. "What do I get if I give you a cigarette?"

"You get lots of shiny tin cans to eat, Goaty," she said snatching the cigarette out of my hand and giggling.

I dove for her giant tits. Jenny smoked the cigarette while I sucked her nipples. Rubbing my face against her tits and stomach made me light-headed. I bit her nipple and she exhaled smoke in a hard little gasp.

Suddenly, Jenny sat up, grabbing my arm.

Did she feel guilty about Irene again?

I stopped sucking her nipples and looked at her. She was staring at my scars.

"Your poor little goat arm," she said sadly, running her fingers over my self-mutilation scars.

I've always wanted people to be horrified when they see my arm full of pink slashes, but now that Jenny noticed, I felt bad that they hurt her.

"They look worse than they are," I said trying to keep Jenny from being sad.

My scars never look as bad as I want them to look. What I really want, but have never had the guts to do, is to give myself a giant scar across my throat. If my throat got slashed, that would be hot. That would get me a girl or two. If I slashed my throat with a buck knife—like the ones that are on the hunting counter at Sears with the black shiny handles and the swooping silver blades—and if I lived through that but talked about it nonchalantly—if I could still talk—if I didn't hit my windpipe—the ladies would love it.

Bo doesn't have to slash himself with razors—Hope loves him anyway. Besides, he has real scars because his evil twin, or some killer, is continuously stabbing him. Hope is so nice to Bo when he gets hurt. My whole life I've wanted someone to be nice like that to me. So far only Jenny has. The only one tougher than Bo on *Days of Our Lives* is Patch. He's not on the show anymore, but he used to get tons of ladies because he had an eye patch and a big scar across his cheek. Ladies love themselves an eye patch. How come the world is separated into two groups: people that cut themselves with razors in order to manipulate other people to love them, and people that fall in love with people who cut themselves with razors because they have savior issues?

"What are the razors for, Francesca?" the police asked when they carted me off to the mental hospital.

Really, what weren't the razors for? The razors are for when Irene puts on lipstick before a date with Gustavo. When Maria kisses Ashanti in front of me. When customers don't leave a tip. After difficult phone calls with the mother. When one of the homeless guys in front of my building gets brought to the hospital. To be carried always in my wallet like a condom.

I started with a small Swiss Army knife, gnawing away at my flesh, afraid to really do some damage and go deep, but the knife was dull and aggravating. So I went looking for something sharper. My father had an old metal razor that he shaved with. If you turned the metal handle, two metal doors slowly opened. Underneath the doors was a new double-edged razor. I remember the first time I twisted the handle and watched the doors open, revealing the shiny, beautiful razor. It was like an Advent calendar for the depressed! Instead of chocolate inside each window, a brand-new razor. I loved watching the razor come into view. That must be how men feel the first time they see a woman climb out of a cake.

I wanted to see blood—my proof that maybe things weren't going well. Who could dispute a bunch of blood?

When I was at the mental hospital, it didn't feel sad the same way mental hospitals feel sad in movies, with everyone sitting around drooling hopelessly on themselves and making macaroni art. There were definitely people drooling, but I guess I knew I'd get out. Unlike the droolers, who weren't going anywhere fast.

Sometimes I use the fact that I was in a mental hospital as a pickup line with girls. I did when I first met Maria. Being dragged to a mental hospital is tough. Deep down I know I'm not tough. If I were really tough I would have escaped from the mental hospital. Believe me, I thought about it—wandering out the front door, and then walking for miles along the highway next to the strawberry fields. It didn't seem like anyone was really watching us. But I was afraid of hurting my mother. I knew I could survive alone, but if you run away, you have to run away forever. In high school I was obsessed with running away. I thought I'd drive my car five hundred miles to San Francisco. This was the car that broke down every other day.

* * *

Sexual abuse victims often cut themselves. I read that in *The Courage to Heal.* Maria's an incest survivor. Everyone's been molested but me. That's how it felt until my mother called to tell me she always suspected that I might have been molested. I racked my brain, looking for the villain. Who did it? Someone in the family? A stranger? The older neighbor boy? Who? Molesters can be family members, and they could have done it for years, *The Courage to Heal* says. Many people have no recollection of being molested, *The Courage to Heal* says. All signs pointed to my molestation. One sign of being a sexual abuse victim is the propensity to self-mutilate.

When I told Maria I didn't know if I'd been molested, she invited me to her art opening.

"It's all about incest," she said. "See how you feel when you're looking at the photographs. If they stir any memories."

Her photographs were of mattresses floating in filthy creeks, women hanging upside down with bandages unraveling off their wrists, mailboxes with broken posts, children sitting in barren dirt lots with dirty shirts on. Had a broken mailbox ever molested me? Maybe I was taking it too literally.

"How did you feel when you were looking at the pictures?" Maria said.

"Sad," I answered. But I felt sad for the children's dirty shirts, not for my own memory of molestation.

"You should read *The Courage to Heal.*"

"I have read it. I'm positive I haven't been molested."

"Try reading it again," she suggested.

22

HOW COME THE serial killer in soap operas always wears black leather gloves and shiny black sneakers? There's always a mystery killer, or stalker, or rapist lurking around—someone's twin brother who's been missing, who comes into town right before a funeral or wedding or birth of an illegitimate child. Hope's had millions of stalkers. She's also married Bo four different times. One time the stalker taunted Bo by mailing anonymous threatening letters to the police station. Bo walked around furious, punching walls. Why she stays with him, I'll never know.

Anyway the soap-opera killer's shiny black sneakers shuffle down the hall, and his leather glove slowly starts to turn a doorknob. At the beginning of the episode he starts turning the doorknob, and fifty-nine minutes later, at the end of the episode, he's still turning the doorknob. OH MY GOD. WHO'S THE KILLER? WHY WON'T THEY SHOW HIS FACE? I CAN'T BELIEVE I HAVE TO WAIT UNTIL TOMORROW TO FIND OUT WHO THE KILLER IS! My grandmother gave up watching *Days of Our Lives* because she went to New York for a monthlong vacation and when she came back some hospital staff hostages were still being held in the boiler room. "Enough's enough," she said. Like Janis Joplin says, "Tomorrow never happens, man. It's all the same fucking day, man." I love Janis Joplin.

Usually a month later the killer's leather glove finally opens the front door of a temporarily blind woman character, and then the show ends with the blind woman hearing the doorknob turn and calling out her husband's name. Up until this point in life, everything told her that the sound of a turning doorknob meant her male provider was home. But this time it would be different. This time she'd be in for a surprise. But who was *this* serial killer and how did he take such good care of his gloves and sneakers? If the serial killer worked at IHOP, Julio would respect him. The serial killer would end up getting all the best brunch shifts just because his shoes and apron were so spiffy.

*   *   *

"What are the razors for, Francesca?"

There were five bloody ones in my wallet when the police picked me up. I didn't know how to explain the difference between self-mutilation and suicide attempts to law-enforcement agents. Police see bloody razors and they don't believe you're using it as a way to impress girls.

When Bo came home with a bashed-in face, Hope always tended to him so sweetly. At first, he'd refuse her help. "It's not that deep," he'd say as the blood coursed down his face.

And after a few worried tears on Hope's part, he'd give in and let her put that reddish-brown iodine on it. Iodine is a poet's dream come true. We didn't have iodine in our house. We only had the dusty, brown, plastic bottle of peroxide that stung and made white bubbles jump up from pools of blood. I remember the neighbor boy climbing over the fence and nicking himself. A real nick. Maybe one splinter. Nevertheless, he sobbed until his mother swept him inside and swabbed his entire arm in iodine. When he came back outside to play, he looked like a lion had mauled him. Iodine turns molehill injuries into mountain injuries. I've wanted mountain injuries my whole life.

23

LAST NIGHT IRENE met me after my shift and we went to the diner next to IHOP for grilled cheese sandwiches. It was only the second time we've hung out alone since Jenny told her we slept together. I was afraid Irene might still be mad at me, but she was in a really good mood. When she laughs she becomes even more beautiful.

After dinner we walked back to Simplicity House along Union Street, stopping to look at the slices of pie inside café windows. When we got to Simplicity House she invited me upstairs for a cup of tea. Upstairs, Gustavo was throwing a tantrum because he hadn't done his political science paper for school.

"I can help you with your paper now," Irene said.

"There's not enough time now," Gustavo yelled. "I haven't even started yet."

Turning to me, she said, "I'll be right back."

She followed Gustavo into their bedroom, where he continued shouting.

I tried to eavesdrop, but all I could hear was Gustavo yelling, "Leave me the fuck alone."

A second later Irene emerged, crying.

"Can I sleep at your house tonight, Goaty?"

"Sure," I answered, totally surprised that for once she wasn't going to stay and process with Gustavo.

Irene wouldn't tell me what happened exactly in the bedroom, but she cried hysterically the whole way back to my apartment. Strangers on the street stared at her, and I felt humiliated to be around such a public breakdown.

When we got to my apartment I made two cups of chamomile tea and settled into bed next to Irene. Irene put her head on my chest and I wrapped my arms around her, petting her stubbly head. I wanted to console her but couldn't bring myself to support her relationship with Gustavo in any way.

"I have to be at work at five-thirty, Goaty. Do you have an alarm clock?"

"Yeah."

I set the alarm clock, turned out the light, and repositioned Irene's head on my chest.

"It's going to be okay," I said.

The next thing I knew, Irene was kissing me hard. I felt utterly confused, like the cashier had given me too much money and when I mentioned the mistake said, "No, keep it, and here's the rest of the drawer, too."

When she had asked if she could spend the night, this was the last thing I was expecting. It felt unnatural to finally be kissing her after almost a year and a half of longing. For the last year and a half, I'd stalked, clung to, worshipped, idolized, lingered near, lied to, petted, and hugged her. I'd expected if we ever kissed or had sex it would be smooth and seamless, a constant flowing where we were both removed from our pasts and weaknesses. Instead, I kept readjusting my mouth so that her mouth didn't feel so hard.

Irene tossed me off her and crawled to the middle of the bed. She was changing into a completely different person. This was sex Irene, curling her lip and cat snarling, at me, on her hands and knees shaking her ass. But she wasn't joking. Thank God the lights were out because I'm sure I looked petrified.

Why was being a cat sexy but never a goat? How come no one ever tried to act sexy by running dopily forward like a goat with floppy ears? Jenny would.

Irene grabbed my hand and shoved my fingers inside her. I moved my fingers in and out of her while she spit on her finger and started rubbing her clit. I was petrified of not fucking her right.

"Move faster," she ordered.

I did, slamming my hand in and out of her. It didn't feel like sex but like some sort of arm-strengthening exercise. My arm was exhausted from fucking her. After a few seconds I realized she'd come and I crawled on top of her, kissing her sweaty neck. The room smelled like sex. For a second, I was afraid she was going to try and fuck me, but she didn't. She got up to pee and then got into bed behind me. The minute her arms were around me, I felt relaxed. I've always felt safe in her arms.

I decided to walk Irene to work the next morning. We didn't say much to each other, but we held hands the whole way to the health food store where she worked. It felt good to be walking Irene to work after we'd had sex the night before, like I'd made some sort of progress in my life as a sexual being. Street hustlers appeared in and out of doorways, people walked druggedly from one fire hydrant to the next, trying to steady their doped-up selves, a few homeless people remained splayed in their urine-soaked clothing in the park, and the rest got in line with everyone at the methadone clinic. When we arrived at the store, neither one of us had mentioned the night before. Irene's workplace is three blocks from Simplicity House. She gave me a hard kiss on the mouth good-bye and walked into the store.

I turned around and started to walk back home, but when I got to the corner where I turn to get to Simplicity House, I turned. Jenny answered the doorbell sleepily.

"Is Gustavo here?" I asked, afraid of a witness.

"No, why? He slept at a friend's last night after the fight with Irene."

Ten minutes later Jenny's nipples were in my mouth. My head flushed with the thought of being in bed with two different women in less than twelve hours. Jenny gave me a hickey on my stomach. For a second I panicked about Irene seeing it, but then I thought I could just say she did it, even though I couldn't remember her biting my stomach. For a second I thought about telling Jenny I'd had sex with Irene. But I was afraid she might be jealous, or even feel betrayed, so I didn't. I went down on her and we both drifted off to sleep. It felt so good to be curled up naked next to her, but I suddenly felt afraid Irene would come home on her break and find me in bed with Jenny hours after she and I had slept together. I slipped away from Jenny, and quickly got dressed. Jenny stirred.

"Goaty, where are you going?"

"I'm going home to write. Go back to sleep."

"Okay," Jenny said sleepily, "call me later."

Did I even have to tell Jenny I'd slept with Irene? Everyone slept in the same bed in Simplicity House, so it isn't exactly clear, when you find two people in bed, what that means exactly. I'd slept in bed with Irene, three months after I'd met her. I'd wrapped my arms around her, I'd seen her without her shirt, all of those things, but I'd never *done it* with her. Now I'd done it. And hours after I'd *done it* with Irene I'd *done it* with Jenny.

I walked home to call Maria. It wasn't so hard to be a lesbian. After all the time I spent alienated in the public library reading depressing books about gay runaways turning tricks and huffing gas, for one moment, I basked in the joy of being gay. Now it would be okay if I died because I'd at least had sex with a few women. Granted, neither one was Hope from *Days of Our Lives,* but I had to start somewhere.

I tried to sleep when I got home, but Irene's scent on the pillow made me toss and turn. I replayed the night in my head. Maybe it hadn't been as awkward as I thought. Maybe I was the one who was the bad kisser. I didn't want to call Maria before eleven because her MS medication makes her sleep late. And I didn't want to call exactly at eleven either, because that's when I usually call her and I didn't want to seem like I always did the same thing. At 11:09 I ran out of willpower and called Maria. Maybe she'll ask me to come get in bed with her and then I can sleep with three women in one day, I thought hopefully. Her answering machine picked up. Goddammit. I really needed to talk to her. My head was spinning.

There was no one left to call. Irene was at work. And besides, I needed someone outside of the love triangle. I thought about telling Jenny the truth about my night with Irene again, but something in my gut told me not to. Should I call William? I immediately nixed that decision. Where was Maria?

I wandered barefoot to the kitchen, trying to grab pills of carpet with my toes on the way, but I was uncoordinated from sleeping so little. There was nothing in the fridge but a tiny bit of peanut butter and seven eggs. On the counter next to the sink were two packages of Top Ramen. It was too early for Top Ramen. What I desperately wanted was to go to the Tumbleweed Café with Jenny and get a bacon cheeseburger, french fries, and a strawberry milkshake. We could smoke and talk about how someday we'd be famous writers. I love smoking in restaurants. It's so much more fun than at home.

Or I could go to Maria's apartment and she could fix me something to eat. I could lay my head in her lap and feel her thick, black hair sweep against my face when she leaned down to kiss me. I wanted to make Maria come like I'd made Jenny and Irene come. I giggled at the absurdity of that thought. I love everyone. I needed a friend to talk to about my sexual exploits. I couldn't believe I was actually using those words about my life without lying. I'd really had sex. Not only had I had sex, but I'd had sex with my philosophy teacher from community college. I'd had sex with Irene.

24

"DID I WAKE you?"

"I'm awake," I answered, deathly afraid that my mother's psychic abilities would be working and she'd know I'd slept with Irene.

"You okay? Are you depressed?"

"Mom, I'm not depressed."

"How's work?"

"It's okay."

"You don't like it as much as you used to?" she prodded.

"It's fine. There are just a lot of stupid rules."

I was anxious to get off the phone in case Maria tried to call me back. I didn't want the line to be busy.

"Everywhere you go in life, there are rules, Francesca. This is a subject that you've always refused to accept. That's why you should think about going back to college. An education will help you get a better job. Your father and I know from experience that it's much more difficult to get a job without a college education."

"I don't want to go to college right now, I want to write."

"Don't get defensive. It wasn't my intention to call and upset you."

Pause. Silence. The inhaling of smoke.

"So, what do you do when you're not working?" she said, fishing for information.

"I go to AA."

"Do you feel like you're having problems again?"

"What do you mean?" I asked, exasperated.

"Do you feel like you're going to destroy yourself with alcohol and drugs again?"

"No, Mom. That's not why I'm going. It's a community, that's all. Where people listen to each other."

"It makes me very sad that you don't feel like you can talk to your father or me. That you feel like you can tell perfect strangers the business of your life but that you can't talk to us."

"I'M TALKING TO YOU RIGHT NOW."

"That's not what I mean. You've always been secretive, and then when I ask you if everything is okay, you yes me to death. You were not okay when you went to the mental hospital and I knew it, I knew it, but no one listened to me. Your father yessed me to death. Everyone yessed me to death."

"Well, I think everyone overreacted—"

"OVERREACTED? YOU WERE CUTTING YOURSELF WITH RAZORS AT SCHOOL. THE POLICE FOUND BLOODY RAZOR BLADES IN YOUR POCKETS. OVERREACTED?"

"That was before. Everything's fine now."

"How would anyone know that? You said you were fine then."

"I'm telling you the truth. I'm fine."

I watched a roach walk across the carpet during the pause in conversation.

"Have you made any friends besides Irene?"

"Yeah, I've met a few people."

I thought about Jenny's nipples, and how happy it made me to be naked next to her beautiful body.

"I'm friends with lots of people," I said.

"Your father and I have to come up to San Francisco for a work soon. We were hoping to be able to have lunch with you and see your apartment."

I felt a pain in my chest and couldn't say anything.

"Well, do you think you'll be able to find time to see us when we come to San Francisco?"

"I have to check my work schedule, but I'm sure there will be some time when we can see each other."

"I just couldn't stand to be shut out of your life," my mom pleaded.

"I'm not going to shut you out." I heard the annoyed tone in my voice and tried to soften it. "I can't wait to see you. But I have to get off the phone and go to work now."

I felt bad lying to get off the phone, but I had to talk to Maria and I didn't want the phone to be busy in case she called. Now I needed advice not only about Jenny and Irene but also about my parents coming to visit.

* * *

Today Jenny and I went to this cute coffee place on Polk Street and read each other our new poems. She had to buy my coffee because I dropped all my money in the wall before she called.

We finished our coffees and as many refills as we could possibly drain from the annoyed waitress before she kicked us out. It felt so good to smoke and smoke and smoke. Jenny slipped her warm hand into mine and then gave me a pull and started running.

"Let's go back to your apartment," she said, pushing me into a closed storefront doorway and kissing me. We kissed for a long time. It felt like the first time I took Valium, a slow, warm, overtaking of the body—the heater gradually warming the entire car. Her fingers stroked the fuzz on my neck very slowly. This was the street I'd dreamed about my whole life, this doorway, this cold San Francisco wind, these nail-bitten hands, this mouth on my mouth. We ran up the street, stopping for intermittent groping in closed storefronts every few blocks along the way until we got to my apartment. Andy was sitting on the sidewalk out front of my house with a few other homeless alcoholics.

·"Hi Andy!" we shouted, running past him.

Normally we stopped to sit and talk with Andy, but tonight we were too wound up from making out in storefronts.

Jenny slammed the door of the apartment shut behind us and started pulling off my jacket and T-shirt. We clung to each other, not saying anything, just kissing and trying not to bite on each other's necks hard enough to leave marks. She breathed into my ear as she passed her nose down my neck and ran those little nail-bitten fingers over me. Jenny is big on ears the same way I'm big on collarbones and necks. Her mouth was everywhere, back and forth so fast I could barely figure out where. We stood there naked in the pitch-black apartment. Jenny sucked my nipples and I stared at the neon sign out my window that said *Jesus is the Light of the World.* I liked to pretend it said *Jesus is the Leg of the Worm.* Jenny got down on her hands and knees and backed me up against the wall. Her hand moved between my legs and her fingers hesitated at the opening of my pussy.

"Not inside, okay?" I said.

"I know, Goaty," she said sadly.

I felt Jenny's nail-bitten fingers trying to dig into my thighs as her tongue moved over my clit.

Ever since I've been talking to Maria about incest stuff, and reading *The Courage to Heal,* I'm afraid to let anyone go inside me because that spurs panic attacks for some victims of sexual abuse. Even though I don't know if I've been molested, I didn't want to find out in the middle of a fun night.

25

I'M SO FUCKING sick of waitressing and all the bullshit that goes with it. Julio yelled at me today because my nurse shoe had the tiniest syrup drip on the sole.

"It's a shoe," I said, "shoes get dirty. Shoes touch the ground."

But in the middle of my shift he made me go into the bathroom and try to wash the syrup off with a paper towel dipped in the pink soap from the hand dispenser. Jesus Christ.

"Customers don't like filthiness, Francesca," Julio said.

"Shoes get dirty, Julio," I said back.

* * *

I was really nervous about my parents seeing my life in San Francisco. I just knew something would go wrong. They came over to inspect my apartment before we headed out to lunch. Thank God, they didn't mention wanting to meet Irene.

My dad seemed properly disgusted by my place. He was silent and pacing, and that said it all really. I cleaned and redecorated a little before they came, putting all my photographs up on the wall. When the buzzer went off, I felt the permanent nervous pit in my stomach deepen. I pushed the talk button on the intercom and out came all the noises from the street below, the wail of sirens, spinning and flowing in circles and someone screaming, "I'll fucking kill you, faggot." I heard everything—the tall box of steel that meant my father had arrived and the nervous twitching of twigs against smooth cardboard that meant my mother was outside, absorbed in wringing her hands.

"Come on up," I called out cheerfully.

I walked back and forth across the length of the apartment, picking up the green oval ashtray, then placing it down again two inches where it had just been. There was a knock at the front door. I was relieved the neighbors who regularly scream and throw each other into the wall were still sleeping. My father wore a beige tweed blazer, white button-down shirt, and navy-blue work slacks, and my mother wore a matching navy-blue skirt and blazer. They were here for a sales convention and we were having lunch. We were grabbing a bite to eat. We were not having nervous breakdowns or arguments or pangs of remorse in our collective chests for the decisions we'd made as daughter or parents. We were going to eat some egg rolls. We've all made choices, and each choice came with a consequence. Con-suh-kwens-iz. The great multisyllabic word.

Who were these people and what are they doing dressed like this in my neighborhood? They'll be robbed, shanked, stabbed. Don't they know how to hold themselves in a neighborhood like this? They need to have a thick, silver, chain wound around their knuckles, like the landlady who showed me an apartment down the block.

"I've got this, I've got this," she said defiantly, curling and uncurling her fingers around the chain, when I asked her if it was safe to walk alone at night.

My father paced the perimeter of my tiny apartment like Rilke's panther.

"Quite the Spartan apartment," he said. "Quite the Spartan apartment."

"What does that mean, *Spartan apartment?*" I asked him.

"What did you learn at that goddamned high school? Spartan, like the Spartans. The Romans. The Spartans," he barked.

"I don't know who they are," I said sullenly.

"The Spartans. The Romans," he repeated, face reddening.

"Just because we didn't learn anything about the Spartans, doesn't mean we didn't learn anything. The Spartans weren't the only people in history."

Were they?

"God. Who cares about the Spartans?" I mumbled.

My mother, the bundle of twigs, collapsed but remained standing.

"Do you think your father and I are shallowsuperficial people, Francesca?" *Shallowsuperficial* was one word.

"I should speak for myself here, I shouldn't speak for your father," the bundle of twigs continued.

"Don't speak for Willy Loman," I thought, the only other salesman I knew besides my mother and father.

"How, I mean how, can you live in a place like this? How?" said the bundle of twigs.

It only took about a minute and a half from the time they arrived to get to this point.

"What's wrong with this apartment?" I asked.

"Jesus Christ. What your mother is getting at is that there are prostitutes on the corner, on every corner for that matter. I literally had to step over a drunk in a box to come into the building."

"That's Andy," I said.

"You know him?" the horrified bundle of twigs asked.

"Yeah, I know him."

"Are you telling me you . . . you're friends with a homeless alcoholic?" she demanded.

"So what if I'm friends with him? Just because he's homeless doesn't make him a bad person."

"And the prostitutes, am I to assume they're close friends, too, Francesca?"

"There's nothing wrong with prostitutes. Why do they bother you so much?"

I lit a cigarette and shook the pack in the direction of the bundle of twigs.

"Let's drop it, Theresa. Obviously Francesca has shit for brains," said Willy Loman, who had quit smoking many years before.

Eventually we left the Spartan apartment and went for lunch at a Chinese restaurant on Fisherman's Wharf. That's the tourist area in San Francisco—I learned that on my first day when Jenny told me about all the different parts of the city. My mother and I chain-smoked while we waited for the food to come, and my father asked me if I planned to work at the House of Pancakes forever.

"I like being a waitress," I answered.

I didn't tell him how much I desired to glide through the room with plates stacked all the way up my arms, forcing customers to stop eating, astonished by my grace and dexterity. The nimble waitress, the gazelle.

"Waitressing leads nowhere," my father said.

"Nowhere," he repeated.

I wasn't brave enough to tell him of my desire to be the gazelle.

* * *

Later that night Jenny and I walked down Van Ness Street smoking and substituting satanic lyrics to popular Christmas tunes. Jenny kept singing, "OHHHHH, the devil outside is frightful, but his fire's so delightful . . ." We cackled the whole way to the Tumble-weed Café.

"How was seeing the family, Goaty?" she said once we sat down at a table.

I started to light a cigarette without realizing I already had one lit. For a second, I questioned smoking two at once and the ramifications of that act. I looked at Jenny's eyes and began to tell her about my father pacing around calling the apartment Spartan.

Jenny got up and slid next to me in my side of the booth. At first she hugged me sweetly, but soon we were feeling each other up at the restaurant. I felt a familiar surge of electricity move through me.

"Do you know the song 'Goaty the Stinky-Toed Reindeer'?" she asked, biting my neck.

26

I'VE BEEN HANGING out a lot with William from IHOP. He moved from West Virginia to California to "get discovered" and meet girls. No one told him movies were made in Hollywood, and half the girls in San Francisco were gay. After work on Friday nights we go to Sparky's and he drinks five or six beers and tries to get the waitresses to talk to him. I eat french fries and watch Polly run around taking orders in her leather suspenders.

Lately, he's been coming over to my apartment unexpectedly, saying he's just passing through the neighborhood. At first I couldn't imagine who would be ringing my buzzer since no one ever did. It was really exciting—maybe it's Irene. Maybe it's Maria. Maybe it's even Hope from *Days of Our Lives*. But the answer kept coming up: William, William, William. Sometimes I'd be working on a poem when the buzzer rang and I'd know deep in my bones, it was William, so I'd sit there still, hoping to just disappear—then the guilt would set in and the image of the lonely Southern aspiring actor who'd finally made it out of West Virginia just to end up in San Francisco working at IHOP with losers like me would make me rise from the typewriter and buzz him in.

After I open my apartment door the first thing he says is, "At least I got good friends like you, Francie."

Then I make him a cup of tea while he sits in the Muffins Muffins chair, tilting back and forth all depressed, talking about how he wants to be an actor. He'll drone on and on, and I'll be practically drooling on myself from sleepiness but he'll keep talking.

We work Sunday brunches together, so he comes by and gets me in his pickup truck to save me the walk. I told him he didn't have to even though it takes an hour to walk to IHOP, but he insists. I really want to buy myself the monthly bus pass, but it's twenty-nine dollars and I keep thinking that it's not a necessity. I mean twenty-nine dollars is what I make in an entire slow dinner shift at IHOP.

* * *

I don't know why it's so hard for me to keep my IHOP dress clean. Maybe because everything at IHOP is covered in syrup. Once I get syrup on my uniform, it's all over, because then everything else sticks to the syrup spot. I try to pick up the dirty dishes carefully, making sure not to let the syrup run off the plate and down my dress. Once Molly was trying to help me clean some syrup off my dress with a wet rag and she started laughing.

"It looks like your frickin' breast is leakin' milk. You look like you're frickin' lactatin'."

I went to the bathroom to look in the mirror and sure enough, there was a giant wet spot on my tit.

"Table nine is ready to order," she said, poking her head into the bathroom.

"Don't worry, I'll just tell 'em you're still breast-feeding and sometimes this happens at work."

Then she shut the door.

When I walk to work, I try to conceal my uniform by wearing

combat boots over my nude stockings and my leather jacket over the IHOP dress. I wad my apron and shoes up into my backpack. I'm not sure how I made the distinction that it was less humiliating to wear the IHOP dress in public than the nurse shoes. There's just no way to conceal white vinyl nurse shoes. If some cute girl sees me on the bus, maybe she'll know I'm not a total dork because I'm wearing combat boots.

At the end of my shift I go into the locker room and change out of my uniform for the bus ride home, because if you walk in my neighborhood at night looking like a waitress, you'll get robbed for sure. I love when I get to rip off the nude-colored pantyhose because I hate how they feel drooping between my legs. I guess if I didn't buy the ninety-nine-cent ones, they might actually have elastic in them and not droop. But it enrages me that I have to spend any money at all on pantyhose, so I always buy the cheapest ones. After I take off my pantyhose, I put on my gray sweatpants and faded black T-shirt and then shove my wadded-up dress, nurse shoes, and stockings into my backpack. As a result, my dress ends up with an awful stench from the combining smells of sweat, syrup, and crotch because when I get home I never remember to empty my backpack.

This Sunday when William came to pick me up, my dress was especially filthy.

"Francie, Julio's gonna kick yer ass if he sees that dress."

The dress was a giant smell stain with armholes and a zipper. We had to be at work in a few minutes.

"What should I do?"

"Try to wipe some of that dried food off with a warsh cloth or something."

I went into the bathroom and began to try and scrub off some of the dried syrup.

"Hurry up," William yelled, "we're gonna be late."

I walked out of the bathroom and said, "What about now, how's it look now?"

There were giant wet spots all over the front of the dress. I looked like I was lactating out the middle of my stomach.

"Julio's gonna kick yer ass! When was the last time you did yer warsh?"

"I don't know, two weeks ago . . . three weeks ago."

William leaned over to smell my dress.

"That dress smells! Gawd! It's stinky!"

"Is it that bad? I didn't think it was that bad," I said.

William came closer and took another whiff.

"GAWD! IT SMELLS LIKE SHIT! Spray that dress with some perrrfume."

I went into the bathroom and got the bottle of *Anaïs Anaïs* my mom had given me for Christmas and began to spray the dress all over, under my armpits and on all the wet food stains. I'd had two days off before this Sunday shift but my dress had remained wadded up with the stinky vinyl nurse shoes and sweaty panty hose since my last shift. Then that morning, I'd dug through the dirty laundry for my other filthy dress, but the dress wadded up in the backpack was actually cleaner.

"How's it smell now?" I asked William, who I could barely see through the cloud of *Anaïs Anaïs* in the air.

He inhaled cautiously.

"Oh GAWD. Oh, it's like a per-fumed garbage can. GAWD. I think I'm gonna throw up, I think I'm really gonna be sick."

We walked downstairs and onto the street.

"What am I gonna do?" I whined.

"Francie, you need to air that dress out. Run up and down this street and get some air in it."

"Do you think that'll help?"

"Anything will help, hurry up, start running," said William, pushing me into the intersection.

I ran as fast as I could up Geary Street. It was seven in the morning and the drag queens were heading home from the bars.

"Run faster, Francie. And flap yer arms. You need to air it out," William cheered from the corner of Geary and Larkin.

I began to flap my arms up and down, my nurse shoes slapping the concrete until I was in front of the XXX sex shop entrance. William was laughing hard.

"All right, now run back towards me as fast as you can and keep flapping yer arms," he called out.

I flapped all the way to where his truck was parked. When we got in, I was breathing really hard, and the bottoms of my lungs burned.

"Roll down the window, Francie. That dress is gonna make me puke."

"Stop it. You're making me feel like shit."

I was so out of breath from running. It made me think I should quit smoking.

"Well, I can't help it if yer dress smells like shit," he answered. "Now, roll down the window."

"It's freezing."

"Yer dress is stinkin' up the whole truck. Roll down the window and hang outside while I'm drivin'. You'll air the dress out more that way. And light a cigarette."

I lit a cigarette, took a drag, and tried to blow the smoke straight down into my chest. The cold air poured into the cab of the truck.

"William, it's fucking cold."

"Francie, that dress smells like dog shit. Gimme a drag of that cigarette."

I took another drag of my cigarette and then handed it to William. So I hung myself out the window from the waist up, my face firmly planted into the San Francisco air. Tears streamed down my face from the cold air rushing into it and my cheeks were properly frozen by the time we arrived at IHOP—only five minutes late for our breakfast shift.

27

THE OTHER NIGHT I was walking down Mission Street after an AA meeting, looking over my shoulder to see if the bus was coming, trying to decide whether to spend the dollar, when I saw this woman trying to yank the phone book off the cable that attaches it to the phone booth. She was beating the sides of the phone booth with her fists, screaming and tugging the phone book as hard as she could. She had a shaved head and I thought, "That woman looks like Irene."

"Whyyyyyyyyyyyyyyyy?" she screamed, "why, why, why?"

Then I realized *it was Irene*. I ran the half block to where she was and grabbed her arm.

"Irene, stop!" I shouted. "What's wrong? What's going on?"

She turned to look at me like it wasn't even strange that in the middle of her psychotic outburst I'd be standing next to her on the street.

"He lied to me. They lied to me," she sobbed.

Instead of feeling jealous or angry that she was crying about Gustavo, I immediately wanted to comfort her. Somehow, I convinced her to let me accompany her on the walk home and she calmed down a little bit, taking deep breaths and extending her fingers in and out, as if she were flicking droplets of water off them.

"They've been sleeping together behind my back. They've been lovers since high school," Irene wailed. "Gustavo and Jenny never told me."

By the time we reached the top of Van Ness Street, Irene was ready to forgive Gustavo and was determined to make him pick her over Jenny. I was worried about her. I pictured Irene stopping at every phone booth on the way home, trying to finish the job of pulling the phone book from the cable.

"Why don't you come over and hang out?" I asked.

I was starting to feel jealous about Irene's urgency to get right back to Gustavo. I couldn't believe Jenny hadn't told me about her history with Gustavo. Maybe she *was* as untrustworthy as Irene said. But then again, I never told her about the time I slept with Irene.

"Fuck them," I said, "come over and I'll make you some tea." I wanted to take care of her like all the times she'd taken care of me when I was suicidal.

"I need to go home. I need an answer from Gustavo, once and for all. I need to know if we're building a life together."

What life was she talking about? I wondered if she ever thought about the night we slept together. What exactly needed to be straightened out? What were we all doing anyway besides being obnoxious hippies, chain-smoking, beating drums, eating gruel, and talking about nonviolence and poetry? Suddenly, this rolling out of one bed and into another felt dangerous and unappealing. At that moment I would've done anything for Irene to say she wanted to build a life with me, alone.

"I need to know that the people in my life want to build community. If Gustavo can't commit to living simply and honestly, then I need to know now," Irene said.

It's obvious Gustavo can't be honest—why couldn't she see that? I'd never witnessed this degree of desperation in Irene before. It scared me that for once I was the more together person.

When we got to Geary and Van Ness, Irene turned to me and said, "Thanks for walking with me. You always make me feel so much better. I'll call you later and let you know what happened."

I watched her hurry up the street. She was literally rushing to get back to Gustavo. That quick desperation scared me.

* * *

After three days of waiting for Irene to call, I gave up and called. She assured me how special I am in her life, but said she can't spend time with me right now because she and Gustavo are in "a healing phase." They're thinking about going to a couples counselor.

"What about Jenny?" I asked.

In addition, Irene told Jenny she couldn't trust someone who continually betrayed her and that Irene needed to have a no-contact rule with Jenny for a while. Even though Gustavo lied to Irene about sleeping with Jenny, too, Irene felt Jenny should've known better, since she's had more therapy in her life than Gustavo.

When Jenny was sobbing and begging Irene to not banish her, Irene said, "It's not about the sex. It's about your inability to tell the truth."

I'm sure Irene never told Jenny we slept together either, so it seemed kind of hypocritical to me. Irene still sees Gustavo as someone she wants to share her life with, but I guess they are going to be platonic.

When I first found out Jenny was sleeping with Gustavo I was mad at her for lying to me. I think I felt jealous, too, because we have such a good time together that it seemed impossible she'd be out looking for that somewhere else, as well. But Jenny's so sweet, I couldn't stay mad—plus, I feel sorry that both Gustavo and Irene blamed her.

As a result of all the drama, Jenny decided to move out of Simplicity House. I told her she could crash with me, but she wanted her own apartment, so I got her an apartment in my building. She's on the sixth floor, too, but in the front. It's a studio like mine, but with a tiny extra room like a closet, so it costs $425 month instead of $395.

I was so happy that she moved into the building that last night I threw her a housewarming party. It was just the two of us with a ninety-nine-cent bottle of grape soda and a pack of Winston cigarettes. I avoided the topic of Irene and Gustavo until Jenny brought it up. She said she still really loves Irene and never wanted to hurt her by lying—she can't figure out why she slept with Gustavo, let alone lied about it.

"We've just been through a lot of shit together, Goaty. I've known him a long time."

There was something in her voice when she said it that made me believe Gustavo had some sort of value.

"I'm so pissed at them both for acting like I'm the fuck-up. But you want to know what's really fucked up? I'm going to miss Irene, Goaty," Jenny said. "She told me she didn't want me in her life because she can't trust me."

I didn't know why but I felt guilty that I was still in Irene's life.

"I trust you, Jenny—you'll always be in my life."

But in the back of my head I wasn't sure if that was true.

28

TODAY IRENE CALLED to ask me if I wanted to get a coffee for the first time since she and Gustavo entered their "healing phase." At first I was pissed, since we've never gone ten days without some sort of contact, but then I felt my heart leap around like a dog about to be walked. Irene told me she was downtown and she'd walk over.

Five minutes after I hung up with Irene, Jenny knocked on the door. She was in a really silly mood, and then before I knew it we were making out. I didn't tell Jenny Irene was coming over because I thought it would make her sad. By the time the intercom buzzer rang, I'd forgotten about Irene completely.

"Who's that?" Jenny said, biting my neck. "William?"

I thought about pretending I didn't know Irene was stopping by, but I didn't.

"It's Irene," I said, avoiding Jenny's eyes.

"Are you serious? Why didn't you tell me she was coming over? I don't want to see her," she said, staring at me hurt.

"Hang on," I said to Jenny, and then I pushed the intercom button, "Come on up."

Jenny pushed past me into the hall.

"Jenny," I pleaded, "I'll call you later, 'kay?"

"*When?* After Irene leaves?" she spat at me.

Fuck. I hated hurting Jenny.

When Irene opened the door, I was rinsing the smell of Jenny off my neck.

"I was ringing the doorbell for a while," Irene said. "What took so long? Was someone here?"

"I'm just running late," I said, sitting down in the Muffins Muffins chair to put on my socks and combat boots.

I hadn't hugged Irene when she came in, which wasn't normal for us. I was pissed that she ignored me for ten days, and deep down I wanted to blame her for the ways I hurt Jenny.

"What's wrong, Goaty?" Irene said.

"Nothing," I took a drag from my cigarette and made sure to blow the smoke out the side of my mouth in a dismissive way.

"You haven't even hugged me and you can't even look me in the eye. It seems like something is going on."

I only saw the hurt look in Jenny's eyes when I told her Irene was downstairs.

The sun was going down fast and the last few moments of diffused light hung in the air. I hated myself. I hated Irene.

I wandered into the kitchen, hopelessly. In the refrigerator was a stick of butter with a piece of Jenny's hair stuck to it and a jar of generic strawberry preserves. The sight of the empty refrigerator infuriated me.

"Francie, if you're not going to talk to me, I might as well leave."

This power felt good. Finally Irene was waiting the same way she'd kept me longing and pining, since the first moment I'd met her. At the same time, the thought of being left alone made me feel terrified. Like the sensation I got when I was at parties or parades—being surrounded by people and still feeling desperately alone. People, people everywhere—not a drop to drink. When I first moved to San Francisco, I went to Café Flore on the weekend to pick up girls, but I was too afraid to even look at them, let alone say hi. So I just sat immobile at my little table, drinking my coffee, eating peach pie, and scribbling furiously in my journal about how no one loves me.

Irene followed me into the kitchen and flipped on the light switch. The fluorescent lamp flickered overhead. I reached past her and snapped it off.

"I can't deal with the light right now, okay?" I said to her.

She turned to leave, retrieving her keys from her pocket in a dramatic sign of "I'm leaving."

"Look—I feel like fucking killing myself right now," I said, pulling an old trick out of the bag. "I want to smash every single one of these fucking glasses into the wall." I stared at the four thrift-store glasses I owned sitting in the dish rack beside the sink.

"So throw them," she challenged. "Go ahead, do it."

I hadn't told her the truth about my feelings since I met her. Why start now? Why tell her I was angry she shunned Jenny or hurt that she chose fucked-up Gustavo as a life partner over devoted me? I was sick of being second-best, and I'd only been recently promoted from third-best, since Jenny was cast out of Simplicity House.

I reached into the dish rack and pulled out a plain pint glass. I felt the cold curve of the glass in my hand.

"Throw it, if you're so angry," Irene repeated.

She'd turned on me. It was no longer a challenge to stop my whining as I'd originally thought. She was now using some unapproved sort of therapy on me. I hated her for always trying to save everyone. What if I didn't want to be saved anymore? I threw the glass into the wall, but not full force. As much as I wanted to hurl it and see the glass shatter into ten billion pieces, I was afraid. I was afraid to disturb the neighbors—the neighbors who fight so loud the police are in the building once a week. The glass bounced off the wall and broke into a few large pieces. I looked at my impotence, the top edge of the glass, lying on the rug in front of the Muffins Muffins chair.

"Throw another one," Irene coaxed.

I kept thinking of Bill the super's green army jacket and the pistol he hid in it in case there was any trouble. In his eyes I'd been a good tenant up to this point. Jenny told me the people in the apartment rental office said great things about me when she used me as a reference. I was an ideal tenant, they'd said. Ideal in an apartment building filled with junkies and wife-beaters. I was the valedictorian of 938 Geary Street. I threw the next glass so hard, it made a hole in the wall.

My hands were shaking. For a second I stood still, admiring the hole in the wall. Irene wrapped her arms tightly around me from behind.

"It's okay, Goaty. Sometimes it's really healthy to break things and get the anger out."

I wanted to buck out of her strong hug, but I stayed and let her pet my head.

"Goaty, you've got the biggest heart of anyone I've ever met," she crooned.

These were the words I'd wanted to hear from Irene my whole life. I couldn't believe she was actually saying them.

"Come on, I'll take you out for a hamburger," she said. "Grab your jacket."

I crushed the broken glass into the carpet with my boot on the way to the closet for my jacket. I literally felt my rage and sadness dissipating.

Irene said we could go anywhere I wanted for dinner, so I picked the Tumbleweed even though I felt guilty going there without Jenny. I prayed the waitress wouldn't say something stupid, like *where's that girl you're always chain-smoking and making out with?* Thankfully, our regular waitress wasn't working.

Thank God, Irene didn't say one chastising thing over dinner about my meat-eating or chain-smoking. I needed to just be loved after breaking the glasses. It was like old times, before she moved to SF, when the two of us would go sit at Denny's for hours and play hangman on napkins.

After dinner Irene said, "Want to go see the sea lions at Fisherman's Wharf?"

"I thought you were too old to stay out this late," I teased.

"I'm only ten years older than you, Goaty. Anyway, Gustavo's studying so I thought I'd stay out of the house."

My heart sunk. Of course the only reason she was hanging out with me was because Gustavo was occupied.

"I should go home," I said. "I was going to wake up early tomorrow to work on some poems."

Irene looked a little disappointed. Good. She needed to know I wasn't always at her beck and call.

"You're welcome to spend the night," I dared her.

"Okay," she brightened. "I'll just need to call Gustavo from your house and let him know I'm not coming home tonight."

I was stunned that for once Irene was picking me over Gustavo. Was Irene sleeping over platonically or were we going to have sex? I felt excited to try and have sex with her again, but then immediately became scared of running into Jenny in the hall with Irene. Jenny was devastated that Irene didn't want to be her friend. Poor Jenny. Thankfully, when we got out of the elevator, I didn't see any light coming out from under her door and I whisked Irene right into my apartment.

While Irene called Gustavo, I brushed my teeth hard in case we ended up making out. Jenny loved the taste of a cigarette kiss, but Irene hated smoking. I lingered in the bathroom because I didn't want to hear Irene having romantic good-nights with Gustavo on the phone.

When I came out of the bathroom, the lights were out and Irene was already in bed. It took my eyes a second to adjust to the darkness as I felt my way past the closet. Glass crunched under my foot.

"Are you already asleep?" I whispered.

"Not quite."

"Is Gustavo mad you're sleeping here?" I prodded.

"Not at all. He said to say hi."

Whatever. I took my combat boots off and crawled into bed with my clothes on. I didn't want her to think I was coming on to her.

Irene curled up behind me.

"Everyone wants to be found, Goaty. The problem is sometimes we get so good at hiding we don't even know we're doing it anymore. You never have to hide from me."

"Okay," I said.

"I want you to be a part of the life I build," she whispered. "I want you to be my primary life partner."

I knew Irene could feel my heart beating out of my chest.

"Me, too," I gulped.

Irene slipped her hand down the front of my pants.

I turned so I could kiss her. Her mouth didn't feel as hard as it had the first time we kissed. She slipped her fingers inside me before I could tell her no.

They felt so good moving in and out of me.

29

I WANT TO lock myself up for three months in a clinic where the only food is carrots and carrot juice. There's this carotene experiment going on and they pay you thirty-five hundred dollars to let them experiment on you. I heard if you eat too much carotene, you turn orange. Maybe I could have an affair.

"Mom, Dad, I'd like you to meet my orange lesbian lover . . ."

The other day at an AA meeting this hot punk girl was talking about how when she was a junkie she supported herself by being a guinea pig in various studies. She got picked for everything: cocaine, heroin, crystal. She even did sleep studies where they woke her up every hour for three weeks. Her entire income came from the back page of the *SF Weekly*. If I had known someone would pay me to drink and take drugs I never would have gotten sober. Everyone has tons of hot sex with each other during studies, because they're so lonely from being locked in the hospital for a month. And the hottest part is they have to hide from all the scientists in order to do it. Isn't that the best thing you've ever heard?

The whole reason I really want to go to the carrot clinic is to see if I can survive even higher degrees of loneliness and to finish this book while I'm there.

Once this drunk, homeless man came up to me and said, "Alcoholism is a disease of loneliness."

I'll drink to that.

I wish I could be trapped in a clinic with Irene. The other day we went to the beach together and it was so beautiful. It was cold. Her ears and stubbled head were so red. I kept jumping up to grab her ears and warm them in my hands. She pulled me to her hard by my jacket collar and kissed me. On the bus ride home from the beach, Irene put her arm around me and I pretended to be asleep against her chest; that way if any kids started calling us dykes I wouldn't have to deal with it.

I'm not absolutely certain that Gustavo and her are solely platonic, but that's what she keeps saying. She said she loves him but she can't rely on someone who is so violent. Then she told me I was the kindest person she ever met, and she needed someone kind to build a life with. I don't want to get my hopes up too high, but who would've thought my old philosophy teacher from community college would want to be my lover?

30

THIS WEIRD GUY has been coming into IHOP lately. I guess
he always comes in, but lately he's been sitting in my section. He's a
three-hundred-pound cop named Tommy and he always orders
either the meatloaf or baked chicken. The first time he got put in my
section I quickly took his order and disappeared because I don't trust
cops. Tommy tried to make jokes with me and Molly was like,
"Ooooh, somebody likes you."

"He doesn't like me."

"Then why does he always sit in your section? Let's face it, the fat
fuck likes you."

"Molly!" I said looking over my shoulder to see if anyone heard her.

"He *is* a fat fuck. Look at him! He's a fat fucking cop."

I walked away but she followed me to the salad bar.

"Why do you think he doesn't drive his own police car?" she said,
"Because he's too fucking fat."

It's true he doesn't drive a police car. He drives a brown sedan
instead.

"He's not a real cop because he got too fucking fat to run
after anyone," Molly said. "It's really hard to get fired if you're a

cop so now all he does is drive around and call in bums and crack whores."

She leaned against the salad bar and smiled at me, in some sick kind of all-knowing way.

* * *

Last Friday Tommy said, "Do you want a ride home?"

On Fridays William usually takes me to Sparky's after our shift but he called in sick last Friday. I knew I'd have to walk home because it had been a slow night and I didn't want to waste any money. Tommy kept asking if I wanted a ride, so finally I just said okay even though I felt like a sell-out to take a ride from a cop. It was better to be a sell-out than to walk home through the freezing wind.

"Have fun," Molly said sarcastically as I walked out the door with Tommy.

He opened my door first and then struggled to fit his body behind the steering wheel. It made me sad that people like Molly made fun of him for being fat.

He floored the gas pedal and we screeched out of the IHOP parking lot. He was going to show me that he was a badass motherfucker.

We drove down Lombard Street saying nothing and then Tommy said, "The department pays me mileage to drive my own car because there's a shortage of police cruisers. I end up making money off it because the mileage allowance is more than I pay for gas."

"That sounds smart," I said.

But it was just a regular car with no cage in the back. What if he caught a criminal? Would they just sit in the backseat like a cousin coming home from the airport?

"It's more undercover this way," Tommy said. "A lot of my patrolling is undercover-type work."

But how can you be undercover if you wear a police uniform? I grasped the door handle as we raced around each corner. Tommy seemed oblivious to his own screeching tires. He went on and on about his "undercover cop" life. In front of us a man was rollerblading in the middle of the street. There wasn't much traffic. The rollerblader weaved in and out of the reflectors in the middle of road like they were a personal obstacle course.

Midsentence, Tommy said, "We've got a live one here."

He reached down near the emergency brake handle, flicking on a bright light. Then he grabbed his CB that was a bullhorn, too, and shouted, "Get out of the road!"

It took me a second to realize the "live one" was the rollerblader. He was rollerblading in the middle of the road, but was still keeping up with traffic. The rollerblader gave Tommy the finger and kept skating. Tommy put his little siren on top of the car and shouted again into the bullhorn again, "Police, pull over, this is the police."

The rollerblader sped up and darted down a side street.

"We'll cut him off up here," Tommy said confidently. "No one gets away from me."

"What did he do wrong?"

"He's not going to give a police officer the finger and get away with it," Tommy said.

I was afraid the car might flip over because we were racing down streets and making sharp turns. The place that Tommy thought for sure we'd nab the rollerblader turned out not to be that good after all because he was nowhere in sight. Tommy darted in and out of a few more streets before he accepted the rollerblader had disappeared. Tommy had let the criminal escape. It all seemed so sad—he was trying to impress me by nabbing a criminal, except he couldn't even find a real criminal. I sat silently.

"I'm not gonna worry about it," Tommy said. "He may have gotten away this time, but I know what he looks like. I'll come across him again. I drive these streets every day." He stretched out *every day* so it sounded like "ehvvvvvvvvvuhreeeeeeeee day."

"I need to swing by the station real quick and then I'll drop you off at your apartment."

I wanted to go home and take a bath so badly that every turn he made down a street that wasn't going to get me there was heartbreaking. Tommy pulled up outside a chain-link fence in front of the police station. On the other side, cruisers were parked neatly in a line. He went in a side door.

His car smelled like French fries. I was hungry but I couldn't see any on the floor. Ten minutes went by. I thought about Jenny. She'd called me earlier in the day and said Gustavo and her were trying to get back together and that they might move to Seattle to start over. She hadn't told Irene yet and I was glad because Irene would get hysterical and I don't know how to handle her when she gets so distraught. Every time the police station door opened, and Tommy didn't come out, I got more enraged.

I wanted to get out of the car and smoke a cigarette, but I was afraid as soon as I did he'd come out. I hate wasting cigarettes. On the other hand, if lighting a cigarette would make Tommy appear, I was willing to start a small fire with the rest of my pack. He was probably standing inside telling the other cops that his new girlfriend was in the car waiting for him.

I smoked three cigarettes before Tommy came outside grinning. "Think I wasn't coming back?" he joked.

"It's been a half-hour," I said. "I need to get home."

My pity for him had evaporated. If I'd taken the bus I would have been home by now.

"Do you have a date or something?" Tommy said, smiling stupidly.

I looked out the window, ignoring him.

"Okay," he said, reversing the car in the same highly dangerous and illegal way he'd been doing all night. Why is it that police officers are always the most dangerous drivers of all? We headed toward the Tenderloin, passing the bus stop I waited at the day I bought my nurse shoes.

"Only six more hours to waste before my shift's over," Tommy gloated.

I turned to glare at him incredulously. When we got to Market Street he made a left, going in the opposite direction of my apartment.

"I live the other way," I said, panicked.

"Oh, I know, I just thought you might want to see a few of the other places that I patrol."

I felt like crying. "I'm really tired."

"Oh, it won't take long. I promise."

His sense of time was clearly different than mine, judging by how long I'd already been in his fucking car. He weaved up and down streets saying things like, "a bum lives in there, but most of the time I look the other way, and you've got the regular hookers on the corner here."

"Wow," I thought, "this is all you have to do to be a cop." I know where all the bums and hookers are, too—I walk by them every day on the way to and from work. I say hi, I bring them sandwiches. We drove by the movie theater with a clock. It was 11:30 and we'd left IHOP at 10:00. I felt myself getting suicidal but I couldn't yell at him to just take me the fuck home.

"There's just one more place I want to show you," Tommy said, pulling up in front of a bar. "I come here every night. They know me real well. Just like IHOP. I just check in and make sure everything's okay. C'mon, I'll introduce you."

"That's okay, I'll wait here."

"Oh, no, I told everyone about you, you have to come in."

He'd told everyone about me? The thought depressed me. The bar was pretty empty. A few people played pool. Tommy said hi and mostly they said hi in the obligatory way that we all say hi to Tommy at IHOP. Because he wore a police uniform, we felt compelled to say hi. Someone got him a cup of coffee.

"Yeah, I have my own coffee cup here," Tommy bragged. "Every night when I come in, I get coffee in my own cup. See, on the side it says, 'Tommy.'"

I felt like I'd been slipped some sort of drug because the evening kept taking more and more surreal turns, all culminating in this moment where Tommy was staring at me and holding up his coffee cup proudly. I nodded catatonically, trying to keep back my tears of frustration.

He introduced me to a few people and bought me a seltzer. Well, he didn't buy me one. He ordered one and the bartender gave him it "on the house." Tommy didn't even leave a tip. I was horrified.

"Yeah, I never have to pay for anything here," Tommy boasted.

He drank his coffee and wandered around the room completely oblivious that the regulars he was trying to make conversation with could care less.

Finally Tommy said, "Well, I better get back to work. I'll look in on you guys tomorrow night."

I couldn't believe he thought the whole night he'd been working.

"The presence of a police officer in a bar always makes people feel a little safer," he said as we got back in the car.

I continued to nod catatonically like the obedient hostage I'd become. What about me attracted the most self-centered, boring men in the world? Do they honestly think I'm straight? I guess everyone looks straight in the IHOP dress.

"You sure you have to go home now?" Tommy asked.

"Yeah, I'm really, *really* tired." The words rushed out of my mouth, a desperate attempt to save myself. "That's my building right there," I said pointing to a building that was eight blocks away from where I actually lived. I didn't want to be in the car another second and I really didn't want Tommy to know where I lived.

He screeched to a stop at the curb and turned off the engine, like we were going to have a conversation. I flung the door open and shouted, "Thanks, bye," before following some stranger into the lobby of his apartment building. The stranger went up the stairs and I pretended to look at the directory for the "guest" I was visiting. I

waited until Tommy's car was gone and then I pulled out my pack
of cigarettes and lit one. There was no sight of Tommy's car, so I
headed back to my apartment.

The streets were pretty quiet except for the occasional prostitutes
leaning against walls and fire hydrants. When I got to my building
I was thankful William wasn't out front. Just Andy sitting on his
little cardboard box with an empty bottle next to him.

"Hi, Andy," I said, but he was passed out.

I stopped for a second, making sure he was breathing. He was.
For a second I thought he was dead.

31

MY MOM CALLED today because she said she had an anxiety dream about me last night.

"Francesca, I had a dream I tried to call you, but a strange man answered your phone and wouldn't let me talk to you."

Over the years my mother's dreamt many things: that she was trying to get into my house but the windows were all cemented shut, that my things were mailed to her in a box and she never heard from me again. She dreamt of earthquakes, floods, and stampeding horses—every possible danger except the most real and imminent: "I dreamt you worked at IHOP and didn't have the self-esteem to quit."

When I was growing up, my mom worked from seven in the morning until eleven at night. During the day she drove around to different companies and tried to sell small electrical pieces that fit inside beepers and computers, and at night she worked at the House of Fabrics. Her car was filled with crumpled hamburger wrappers and watered-down cups of soda with cigarette butts floating in them. Work papers were scattered all over the backseat. The car was a stench of cigarettes, just like Roxanne's.

My mom had to get up at 5 A.M. for work and her alarm clock

blared down the hall to my room. She'd be snoring really loudly next to the clock radio, which had the volume cranked up when I came to see why it was still going off ten minutes later.

"Mom . . . Mom," I'd say, shaking her until she woke up.

My mom and I both wake up startled, like someone's put a gun in our faces and threatened to kill us. It's a panicked, disoriented, gasp thing.

"Your alarm clock's been going off for ten minutes," I'd tell her and she'd say, "Okay I'm getting up." But once I left she'd hit the snooze button and fall back asleep.

Then the next time the alarm went off, I'd go back in to wake her up and she'd act like she was getting robbed again.

In the mornings when she got ready for work, she'd wear a ratty old turquoise terry-cloth bathrobe that was too long for her. Cigarettes burned in several ashtrays around the bathroom as she put her makeup on and got dressed. One day shortly after I'd been arrested and taken to the mental hospital, I walked to the door of her room and she was smoking and sitting on the end of her bed, ashing into the palm of her hand. I knew she was already late for work.

"Mom?"

"What?"

"Are you okay?"

"What does that mean, 'okay'?"

"Are you going to kill yourself?"

"Why? Are you going to kill yourself?"

"No."

"Are you sure?" she said, taking a drag of her cigarette.

"Yeah, I'm sure."

My mother blew the stream of smoke out the side of her mouth.

"I'm not going to kill myself," I repeated.

"Then I'm not going to kill myself," she said. She went into her bathroom and started to put her makeup on.

* * *

I feel like everybody's mad at me. This morning I called Maria and told her everything that's been going on. She said if I was going to try and be life partners with Irene, then I should tell Jenny we shouldn't sleep together anymore.

"Do you love Jenny?"

"I love her, but I think it's just a sex thing. We have really good sex."

"Well, that's good," Maria laughed. "Are you having safe sex?"

"No."

"You need to be really careful, especially if Jenny's sleeping with Gustavo, too."

"She's only sleeping with him sometimes."

"It doesn't sound like anyone knows who's sleeping with who," Maria warned.

She sounded pissed. When I hung up the phone I promised her I'd have safe sex from now on. I hope she doesn't think I'm a total loser now.

Jenny's been getting more and more upset when I spend time with Irene, so I told her maybe we should just be friends. I don't want to hurt her, and I have been. She seemed fine with being just friends, which kind of hurt my feelings. I guess I wanted her to beg me to still sleep with her. And of course ever since I said we should just be friends, I've wanted to run down the hall and make out with her.

Last night Irene spent the night and in the middle of the night when she got up to pee she cut her foot on one of the broken glasses I still haven't picked up. She was so pissed off.

"I'm not sleeping here anymore unless you clean up that mess."

Every time I look at the shards, I feel overwhelmed. I don't know why I haven't cleaned them up.

32

TONIGHT AT WORK this guy named Sal came in wearing a black motorcycle jacket with a silver dragon pinned to the front. He parked his black Harley with green flames on the sidewalk out front. I've always loved motorcycles. My mother never let me have a scooter or motorcycle when I was growing up because she thought I would end up killing myself. Sal and I talked for a minute or two about his motorcycle before I sat him down in Holly's section. When he was leaving, he asked me if I wanted to go for a ride sometime.

"Sure."

"What about Friday?"

"I have to work until ten o'clock."

"I'll pick you up after your shift."

I'm not sure if it's a date or not, but I don't care. I just want to be on a motorcycle so badly.

I tried to make Irene jealous by telling her that some guy had asked me out at IHOP.

"I'm going out with this bad-ass biker on Friday. He has a Harley."

"That doesn't sound safe," Irene said.

That was exactly what I wanted her to say.

"Who wants safe?" I laughed.

The night of our "date," Sal waited in the lobby with his leather jacket on while I did my tickets.

"Just give me a second to finish and change out of my uniform," I said.

"Okay." He smiled.

When I was done I ran to the locker room and quickly pulled off my uniform, wadding it up into my backpack. I pulled on my sweatpants, T-shirt, and combat boots. Then I slipped into my leather jacket that was just like Sal's. Julio and The Big Boss stared at me as I rushed by them. Sal suddenly looked disappointed.

"What's the matter?" I asked.

"Nothing. You just look *really* different in your uniform."

Oh my god, this sick motherfucker prefers me in the IHOP dress.

"Everyone looks *different* in the IHOP dress," I said.

We went out to the parking lot where his bike was parked, and he signaled for me to get on behind him.

"Don't put your hands on my shoulders, I can't steer that way. Put them around my waist."

The motorcycle was so loud and I could barely hear him speak as we tore down Lombard. We weaved up and down the Marina streets for about fifteen minutes and then he pulled back into the IHOP parking lot.

"Would you kill me if we ate here?" he asked.

"Yes."

"I'm craving diner food," he said.

"Anywhere but here, Sal. Let's keep going on the motorcycle."

My ears were freezing from the wind because we weren't wearing helmets, so I buried my nose into the back of Sal's leather jacket and inhaled. It felt good to be going fast. Sal pulled into a diner a few blocks down from IHOP. I was sad the ride was over, but I guess I couldn't expect him to drive me around all night.

"Thanks for taking me on the motorcycle."

"Did you have fun?"

"Oh yeah, I love motorcycles. I've always wanted one."

"Yeah?" Sal asked.

He kind of had the same inquisitive look on his face he got when he saw me come out to the lobby in sweatpants.

The diner was packed, but the people eating there seemed a lot cooler than the ones that come into IHOP after hours. The hostess told us the wait was forty-five minutes but she could get us a coffee if we wanted to wait on the bench outside.

"We'll wait," Sal said.

Outside on the bench I pulled out a cigarette and Sal lit it for me.

"Such a gentleman," I said sarcastically.

"So," Sal started.

"So what?" I asked.

He chuckled.

"What are you laughing at?"

"Why'd you go out with me tonight?" he asked.

I hesitated, wondering how to breach the topic of me being a dyke. "I wanted to go on a motorcycle ride and you didn't seem like a serial killer. Why did you ask me out?"

"Because I wanted to fuck you."

I laughed out loud. "Oh. Uh. That's really a nice thing to say. But I'm kind of into women."

His face froze for a second and then he said, "Oh. Okay. That's cool."

"But I still had fun on the motorcycle."

Telling him I was gay was all Sal needed to launch into his plethora of personal sex conquests.

"Once I was on my motorcycle and I saw these two hot girls hitchhiking. They were so hot. So I pulled over and asked them if they wanted to party. Okay, they said. So I brought one of them back to my house while the other one waited on the side of the freeway. Then I went back and picked up the other one. It wasn't far from my house. They were lesbians, but they fucked men, too. When we were all inside my apartment, I went to get some beer out of the refrigerator and they started making out in front of me. This was before I quit drinking. I'm in AA now—"

"I'm in AA, too," I said, excited. Why couldn't I ever meet anyone cool like Sal in AA?

"That's cool," Sal said, basically ignoring me. "So the girls were making out and then they started stripping for me. After a little while one of them reached over and started to unbuckle my belt to take off my pants, and I was like, well I better tell them I only have one leg, so they don't get a surprise."

"You only have one leg?"

"Yeah," Sal said, "I lost the other one in a motorcycle accident."

"God. That's terrible. And you still ride a motorcycle?"

"I'll never get motorcycles out of my blood. So the girls are wasted, and they start trying to help pull off my fake leg. Then, get this, they start rubbing up on my stump. They were so into it, they both were rubbing all over it."

"What luck," I said, horrified.

"Yeah, yeah," Sal said. He had that faraway smile of fond memories. "So, that's a long story to tell you why I asked you out."

"Oh yeah. I definitely see the similarity," I teased.

"You just seemed kind of wild."

There was something really endearing about Sal. For a split second I contemplated fucking him. I'd show Irene she wasn't the only person who could fuck a guy. But when I tried to imagine fucking Sal, the only thing I could picture were the lesbian hitchhikers writhing on his stump. He had to be lying about them. Who would go through all the trouble of going back to pick up the remaining hitchhiker on the motorcycle? Sal would, that's who.

Finally, the hostess seated us at a table. We unfolded our menus and began looking. I was starving.

"Excuse me," two girls who were seated at the next table over called to us, "do you know what the stars mean on the menu?"

Next to some items on the menus were stars. On the bottom of the first page there was a legend. "A * next to any entrée denotes a new menu item." I pointed this out to the girls.

Both girls had long blond hair and looked like hippies who sold jewelry in parking lots at Grateful Dead shows.

"Hey," Sal said, to the rattier of the two girls, "you're the waitress from Sparky's, right?"

"I quit, thank god."

"I remember you, we used to come in all the time. Me and my friend Tom. The big guy with the black mohawk."

"Oh, I know who you're talking about," the ratty girl said, "he kind of looks like you but he has a tattoo of a spiderweb on the side of his head."

"Yeah, it's a black widow. I went with him when he got it."

The girl and Sal started to reminisce, forgetting we were there.

The other hippie looked at me and smiled sympathetically.

"Where do you work?" she said.

"At IHOP," I said. "Are you a waitress, too?"

"No, I'm a therapist."

She didn't look like a therapist.

"I need a therapist," I almost shouted, bolting out of my seat.

Sal and the ratty hippie overheard me, looked over and laughed.

"Did you know that if you cut up the word *therapist*, it spells *the rapist?*"

She smiled warily.

"Anyway, when I first moved here I went to this sliding-scale therapist at OPERATION COMFORT ZONE. What a car wreck she was," I blurted. "I was like 'hi, I really want to kill myself' and basically she said go play ping-pong at the gay youth center. I'm lonely, I told her, but I'm not that lonely."

The hippie therapist handed me her card and said, "Well I'm just starting out so I have a sliding-scale fee if you need one. Call me if you want.'"

"Thanks," I said, taking the card. Her name was Star.

"And I promise not to tell you to play ping-pong," she said, smiling.

Was she flirting with me? She was kind of cute, even though I wasn't usually attracted to Dead Heads.

The waitress came over. "Sorry about the wait," she said, "are you ready to order?"

"I've been a bad boy," Sal said, giving this kind of half-charming smile, "I haven't even looked at the menu yet."

He must have a waitress fetish, and our waitress actually seemed charmed.

"I'll be back in five minutes. And you better be ready," she said playfully.

Sal seemed fine flirting with everyone in front of me. I guess after I told him I "was kind of into women," the understatement of the year, he was going to make the most of the night, however he could.

I ordered the grilled cheese because it was the cheapest thing on the menu and I wasn't sure Sal was paying for me now that he knew I was gay. Sal got a steak sandwich. The hippies went back to talking to each other.

"So, how long have you been in AA?" Sal asked.

"Since I was seventeen and got dragged to a mental hospital. The cops arrested me at school and I had to go to an AA meeting every day in order to graduate. I stayed sober two and a half years, but then I got drunk."

"Why?"

"I was in love with this woman. I moved here to be with her. Well I didn't really move here for her, but I moved here because all I could do was think about her after she moved. I wrote her letters every day on my lunch break."

"So you got drunk with her?" Sal asked.

"Oh, no, I was working at Tower Records and we'd always go to someone's house after work. Everyone but me drank. I'd just drink soda, or cranberry juice, and watch everyone get fucked up. But one night I said, fuck it. It was so hard to take that drink. Like I didn't even want to do it, but I made myself. Next thing I know it's five in the morning and I'm throwing up and hitchhiking, just like old times."

"You gotta stay away from people who drink," Sal warned. "And you gotta work the steps. Have you done the fourth step?"

"Yeah. The hardest thing I ever had to do was tell my first sponsor I was gay. And you know what that fucking pervert said? I finally get the courage to tell someone my big secret—the core of all my pain, right, and he says, 'Oh everyone has fantasies about people of the same sex, it doesn't mean you're gay.'"

"Whoa. So your big secret was that you were gay?"

"Yeah. Towards the end of my drinking, when I got really sloppy, I was afraid people would find out because I was always sobbing and being all intense with women at parties. When I got sober, I was like oh, that's why I was stalking girls and telling them their collarbones were beautiful."

"Collarbones are a really pretty part of a female," he said. "So now are you girlfriends with that woman that you drank over?"

"Um. Kind of. It's a long story."

Sal was wrestling with a piece of steak that had come out of the sandwich. It dangled from his mouth.

"I have a secret I've never told anyone," he confessed. "When I did my fourth step I didn't have the courage to tell my sponsor about this one thing."

Sal looked over at the hippies, who were deep in conversation and eating their cheese fries. He lowered his voice to make sure they wouldn't hear.

"Sometimes it just gnaws at me," he said.

Oh my god, he killed someone.

"It's probably just grown into this big thing in your head," I said hopefully.

"No, it's a big deal."

He did kill someone.

Sal looked around the restaurant in the inconspicuous way that only makes people look conspicuous.

"I'm gonna tell you, because I want to get this off my chest once and for all."

"You'll feel better, after you tell me," I said, but then I thought about when I told my first AA sponsor I was gay. Whatever Sal told me, I promised myself I wouldn't dismiss it the way my sponsor had. He glanced back at the girls, who were involved in their conversation.

Sal whispered, "I made out with a transvestite."

I stopped myself from laughing. This was the big secret? I tried to remember to be nurturing.

"Oh," I said.

"But I'm not gay."

"That's cool."

I chose my words carefully.

"Lots of people make out with transvestites."

"No," Sal said, "I liked it. I got turned on."

"Sal, maybe—"

"I don't want to talk about it anymore. The important thing is I got it off my chest." He seemed depressed.

The girls next to us finished eating, and Star told me again to call if I wanted. Sal paid for the meal, which I was really grateful for because I'd only made forty-eight dollars at work and normally on Fridays we make at least seventy dollars, but now I was sorry I hadn't ordered meat.

"Well, at least you finally told someone your big secret," I said in the parking lot.

"You're not gonna say anything to anyone, right?"

"Who would I tell?"

"Well, like if Star becomes your therapist . . ."

"I promise I won't tell anyone," I said, trying to imagine myself in therapy working through Sal's demons instead of my own.

Sal truly looked despondent and said he was going to hit his midnight AA meeting so he couldn't give me a ride home.

"That's okay," I said, disappointed. I'd have to take the bus instead of getting another motorcycle ride. He gave me a hug.

"Here's my number," he said, "Maybe we can go to a meeting sometime."

"Sure, thanks for the grilled cheese."

He revved his motorcycle loudly and then ripped out of the parking lot. I lit a cigarette and headed toward the 38 Geary stop.

33

A FEW DAYS after I went out with Sal I got the courage to call Star. It felt weird to be calling her but there was no way she could be worse than the therapist I had at OPERATION COMFORT ZONE. We made an appointment and I felt nervous and excited, simultaneously. I don't want to get better so quickly that I stop writing this book.

When my mom called I told her I was going to see a therapist. What a mistake that was. She sounded like she was about to cry.

"I don't understand why you can't talk to your father and me about your troubles. Don't you understand that your father and I would give up our own lives in order to save yours if that situation, god forbid, came up?"

"Mom, I wouldn't want you to give up your life for me."

"Well, I *would* give my life up, Francesca. Besides, how can you afford a therapist?"

"She's a sliding-scale therapist."

"I don't know what that means."

"It means you pay only what you can, based on your income."

"No matter how much it costs, it's going to be more than you can afford—you don't even have money to take the bus."

"I have the money to take the bus. I'm just trying to save money. Anyway, I like walking."

"Your father and I wouldn't charge you a thing to talk about your problems."

I felt guilty for making my mom feel excluded, but I certainly couldn't hire her as my therapist. I wasn't that unhealthy yet.

*   *   *

Today was my first appointment with my new therapist and I like her a lot. She had me tell her my entire life story in fifty minutes. Life stories always sound worse in therapy, since everyone focuses on the bad things.

Star kept saying about Irene, "So she was your teacher, and she has two other lovers that were also her students."

I told her Irene wasn't having sex with Gustavo and Jenny anymore, and that she wasn't even speaking to Jenny, but that Gustavo and her lived together platonically. They're like family. People seem really tripped out by the fact that I'm dating my old philosophy teacher. But I think that's because they don't really think about what it means to live simply and nonviolently.

When I told Star I cut myself she asked if she could see my scars. I showed her most of them and she made me promise that no matter what, if I felt like killing myself I had to call her first. One of her clients had recently killed themselves without calling her first and she was still reeling from that.

"I won't be able to see you as a client unless you agree that you'll call me *before* you try to hurt yourself. This is my home phone number. You can call anytime day or night. Can you promise you'll call me before you act on any suicidal urge?"

Star looked like she was going to start crying. I felt so bad for her.

"Yeah. I can promise."

34

THE OTHER DAY I went to see if Jenny wanted to take a walk with me and I heard her and Gustavo having sex inside her apartment. Thank god I didn't knock on the door. I didn't tell Irene about it because I know it would open up all those old wounds for her. Irene is going back to teaching at the community college now that her sabbatical is over. She wants to teach just Tuesdays and Thursdays so she can fly up to San Francisco and see me for long weekends. I'm going to miss her a lot because we've been having such a great time together lately.

* * *

I went straight to an AA meeting after my Sunday brunch shift today. The poofy sleeves on my IHOP dress are just long enough to cover my self-mutilation scars, but my sleeve must've got pushed up when I took my jacket off and I didn't notice all my scars were visible. So I was sitting in the back of the AA meeting wanting to say how badly I've wanted to drink lately, when I see this really skinny guy next to me looking at all my scars. He had acne pockmarks all over his face and was wearing a black skull bandanna tied over his greasy hair.

"I cut my arms, too," he whispered in a real tough way. "Let's get coffee after the meeting."

AA members are encouraged to go out with each other for coffee after meetings to share their experience, strength, and hope. Maybe this will help me stay sober.

"Okay," I said, even though I thought he was really creepy.

We went to this horrible chain restaurant that's even worse than IHOP. The place was decorated all in brown, and specialized in pies.

I listened to him tell tale after tale of rocker chick girlfriends, booze, and heavy metal bands that never made it. He was a failed musician. Who wasn't? I had a dusty blue kazoo and silver harmonica waiting for me on my kitchen shelf as we spoke.

In the middle of his ranting about a lead singer that fucked him over, he leaned across the table and said, "You're fuckin' pretty, you know that? You don't need no fuckin' makeup."

I stared at him, not knowing what to say.

After we finished our coffee creepy skull guy proposed we take a walk. My better judgment told me no, but I went anyway, believing if this whole experience didn't get me raped or killed it would help me stay sober. We walked past IHOP. I was still wearing my uniform with my black leather motorcycle jacket, which was a turn-on to a guy like him.

He suggested we take a walk in the park. Now I began to wish he would try to slit my throat and throw me into a hedge so I could start running as fast as I could to get away from him. Anything to put an end to this excruciating night. Like most guys he never asked me about my own terrible alcoholic past or if I had been in a failed heavy metal band myself that had got a raw record deal.

When I wasn't thinking about getting murdered and which way I'd run if he tried to rape me, I was thinking about my apartment. It was all mine—roaches, lawn furniture, and all. It sat waiting for me and was far more interesting than this freak.

Creepy guy rambled on, inviting me back to his house.

Finally, I managed to do what I'd been trying to do the whole time we were walking—which was to steer him toward the bus stop so I could say, "Gotta go," instead of, "You are boring the shit out of me and freaking me out."

"Here's my number," he said, "call me and we'll hang out again."

"Okay."

The night ended. I lived.

* * *

I called the suicide hotline tonight. I know I should've called Star but I was afraid to worry her. I've never been closer to actually killing myself. I don't know how to explain it except to say every time I think I'm free, I discover another layer of myself riddled with lies and fear. I know it's a bad idea to have Maria as my sponsor, since I'm so obsessed with her, but I don't want to lose her. The bottom line is I can't be honest with people I like, so how am I going to do my fourth step? Basically, I have to tell her all the things I've never told anyone. All the times I lied. All my secrets. Even that I love her. That's what started my whole suicidal panic.

I fell in love with Maria because I was trying not to love Irene, and now I love them both. Maybe everyone in AA is in love with their sponsors. It just kills me that she has MS. If I could have MS instead of her, I would. I would have MS in a second if it would make hers go away.

The other thing is when I think about Irene actually leaving, I feel terrified. It's the same terror I felt when she was about to move to San Francisco and leave me behind. We've been getting along so well lately. She wants me to go with her to Southern California for a weekend trip and help her get settled. And she said the hardest thing about leaving San Francisco is leaving me. Maybe things with Gustavo are really over once and for all.

35

"ANDY WAS SO fucked up last night when I got home from work," I said to Jenny on the phone.

It felt weird to be calling down the hall, but we both got into the habit of it now, calling, instead of racing over in T-shirts and underwear. She didn't want to run into Irene and I didn't want to run into Gustavo.

"Is he okay?" Jenny said.

"I've never seen him so wasted. I want to bring him to AA with me, but I know he won't come. So I just keep buying him alcohol because I can't stand to see him sick."

"I know," Jenny said. "I do the same thing."

I missed her sweet voice. We haven't hung out that much recently.

"Do you want to come over?" I asked.

"Yeah, I'll be right over."

Jenny gave me a big hug when she came in the door.

"I've been smoking my brains out," she said.

"Me, too."

"Goaty, I have some big news to tell you."

I was sure she was going to admit to having sex with Gustavo again.

"What?"

"I'm moving . . ."

"Where?"

"To Seattle. With Gustavo. My aunt lives there and we can stay with her until we find a place. It will be really good for us to try and start over somewhere new."

The thought of Jenny leaving San Francisco made me so sad.

"Don't leave me," I said, grabbing for her hand. I'd really miss our smoking and gossip sessions. "Gustavo's crazy, Jenny. No offense."

"I know, Goaty. But I really love him, even though he's fucked up. We've been through a lot together."

Her eyes looked really sad. I wanted to save her from all the pain she'd ever felt in her life and all she would continue to feel living with Gustavo.

"Are you sure?"

"Maybe it's a mistake, but I have to try one last time with him. I want to finish what we started without anyone else involved. None of the bullshit with Simplicity House or Irene and him."

"Does Irene know?" I asked cautiously.

"No, not yet. We're going to tell her together, but I'm really afraid."

I thought about having to deal with Irene after she found out this news, and my stomach immediately started churning.

"When are you moving?"

"I told Bill I'd pay rent up to the thirtieth."

"But that's only two weeks away."

"I know, Goaty, but I need the rent money to move and Gustavo is going to have to find a new place when Irene leaves. In fact, that's how this all happened. He came over to my apartment one night to ask me if he could crash with me until he found a place to live and then one thing led to another. He told me he was still in love with me—that we should get back together."

That must've been the night I heard them having sex.

It would be just like old times, Gustavo said, before all the love triangles. Jenny seemed apprehensive.

"What if Gustavo gets violent again?"

"Part of the deal is that when we get to Seattle he has to go to therapy and we both have to start couples' counseling."

"Oh, Jenny. I hope it all works out. I'm going to be lost without you."

"I'm going to miss everything, Goaty—smoking and going to the Tumbleweed, and of course fooling around . . ."

My heart felt heavy at the thought of Jenny leaving. I'd never met anyone before who was so simultaneously silly, deep, and kind.

"How about one kiss for the road?" Jenny said, pulling me to her by my belt loops.

What Irene doesn't know won't hurt her. I leaned forward and kissed Jenny. She kissed me deep, pushing her tongue into my mouth and sucking on the tip of my tongue. After a few minutes, we both came up for a breath. I could've easily had sex with her right then. What's wrong with me? Am I a total whore? I looked into Jenny's eyes.

"I guess I should go before we get into trouble," Jenny said.

"I'm gonna fucking miss you so much."

I didn't want to let her go.

* * *

Yesterday I was walking down Valencia Street to the women's AA meeting, alternating between smoking and playing my harmonica. The soles of my boots are worn down, so each time I took a step, I could feel a nail drive into my heel. I want to be the best harmonica player in the world.

One of my father's favorite jokes was, "You couldn't carry a tune with a wheelbarrow."

Out of nowhere this drunk, homeless guy stopped me to say I was playing the harmonica wrong.

"You gotta blow into each hole individually instead of all of them at once. Here. Gimme your harmonica and I'll show you how to bend a note," he slurred.

It was cool. Except after he gave me the harmonica back I didn't want to put it to my mouth because it was all slobbery and smelled like malt liquor—but I didn't want to be rude either. All of his saliva was dripping out of the harmonica holes into my hand.

"Come on, you try it now," he said.

It smelled so fucking gross but I didn't know how to get out of putting the harmonica up to my mouth because he kept walking alongside of me. Finally, I put the harmonica to my lips and tried to bend a note. I could taste malt liquor on my lips.

"Pretty good, pretty good. Now just keep practicing."

He stopped at the bus stop and when I was sure he couldn't see me anymore I wiped my mouth off with the bottom of my shirt. For the rest of the day my mouth felt dirty even though I kept wiping it off.

* * *

On Jenny's last night in San Francisco, we went to the Tumbleweed. Afterward we sat outside the apartment building for a long time with Andy, smoking cigarettes and saying our good-byes.

Andy kept telling me, "Once I clean up, not now, but once I clean up I want to take you out to dinner."

It was so sweet. He told me he used to be married until his house burned down and now his wife and kids don't talk to him. He always carried their pictures in his little shopping bag, but once his shit got stolen and now he doesn't even have a picture of them. It had never occurred to me what his life had been before this. Of course homeless people don't start off homeless, and some actually have wives and children.

Jenny hugged Andy good-bye and we went upstairs to my apartment. I wanted to make out with her really badly.

"Irene really loves you," Jenny started.

"Really?"

"I see her face when she looks at you."

"She doesn't look at me like she looks at Gustavo," I said bitterly, forgetting that Jenny and Gustavo were together now. "Sorry," I added, realizing I'd hurt Jenny.

"It's okay. I know how Irene looks at Gustavo."

Jenny lit a cigarette.

"Goaty, who are you going to hang out with Irene goes back to school and I'm gone? You're going to be all alone."

"I'm going to work on my book, and I'll probably hang out with William even though he drives me crazy."

"I wish you could come with me to Seattle."

"Me, too."

But I didn't want to move to Seattle. I just didn't want to say good-bye to Jenny.

36

IRENE SPENT HER last night in San Francisco sleeping with me at my apartment. I'm still not used to how she changes into the cat person when we have sex—it's kind of terrifying, the crawling around and hard, seductive looks. Still, in the morning I was sore from fucking. Since it was our last night together I didn't want to waste time sleeping. I fell asleep with my head on her chest and her arms holding me like she did before we'd ever slept together. Before I moved to San Francisco, before I slept with women.

In the morning we went to the diner across the street and had banana pancakes and coffee. Even though I was sick of pancakes I ordered them because they were cheap. Every time I looked at Irene I'd burst into tears. The reality of her leaving was hitting me hard. Since we met, I've spent so much time trying to hide how I feel. Hiding my love for her at the community college, hiding my jealousy toward Gustavo, hiding my affair with Jenny, hiding my terrible want for her to be mine only, trying not to cry in front of her, trying to seem distant, trying to find other people to love so that I didn't have to deal with the fact that I couldn't have her. Whenever the waitress came over to refill my coffee, she'd fill it quickly, then

dart off because I'm sure I looked crazy, sobbing and convulsing. I
hate crying in public.

Andy took me to this diner once after he got his GA check. One
day I came out of my apartment and he was sitting on top of his
black plastic garbage bag with a big smile on his face.

"I want to take you out for breakfast."

"That's sweet," I said because he always said he wanted to take
me on a date once he got his life together.

"No, I want to take you on a date this morning," he said. And
then, "Well, not a date. I want to buy you breakfast for always giving
me food and cigarettes."

He wouldn't let me refuse him so we walked across the street to
the diner. The waitress recognized me from the few times I'd gone
there with Jenny or Irene but she scowled at Andy with his trash bag
slung over his shoulder. Still, she let us sit down. We slid into one
booth and she dropped off two menus and a gold tinfoil ashtray.

"Coffee?" she offered.

"I'll have coffee," I said.

"I want coffee and a beer."

It was probably seven in the morning.

"Did you see how she looked at me?" Andy said. "Like I don't
have money to pay. I've got money. I just cashed my GA check," he
said, taking out some crumpled twenties in his filthy hand.

The waitress came back with the coffee and asked us what we
wanted.

"I'll have the banana pancakes," I said, lighting a cigarette, then
pushing my pack toward Andy. I felt protective of him.

The waitress didn't want him in the restaurant and it seemed like
the only reason she hadn't kicked him out was because he was with me.

"Order some meat," Andy said.

"I just want the pancakes."

"Don't worry about the money, I have money. Get some meat.
They have ham or bacon or sausage."

The waitress looked at me, waiting.

"I just want the pancakes and the coffee," I repeated.

"Bring her some bacon, too, with the pancakes. And here, I'll pay for it all now," he said, handing her a twenty.

We ate quickly after the food came. Andy could hardly eat because he needed a drink so badly his hands were shaking too hard for him to hold a fork. When we were done he slid his garbage sack out of the booth and walked back across the street to the doorway where he slept.

"Thanks for breakfast," I said.

"I wanted to do this for a long time," he said.

The whole way up in the elevator I kept thinking of him saying, "Order the meat, I have money," and it almost broke my heart.

Irene squirmed in her seat and took out a twenty-dollar bill for breakfast. I had two days' worth of tips in my pocket because I wanted to treat her before she went down south.

"Let me pay," I said.

"No, Goaty. I'm going to be making good money at this job."

"But I want to pay."

"You can take me out to dinner another time," she said, pushing the twenty to the edge of the table. "I better get on the bus now."

God, she was leaving. My chest tightened again.

"I'll ride to the airport with you," I said and I felt that familiar second of euphoria from buying myself more time with Irene. I used to feel it a lot when I followed her around the community college and I could talk her into letting me hang out in her office or sit next to her in the booth at Denny's.

I threw my cigarette into the filthy curb in front of the diner, and we got on the bus. Irene struggled with her bag, dragging it to a few empty seats in the back. I held her hand the entire bus ride. Why was the ride to the airport only twenty minutes? Why couldn't it have been six hours? If I could just have six more hours of holding her hand. At the airport, I helped her out with her bags.

"The bus back is right across the street where those people are," she said.

"I'll wait with you until your plane leaves."

When I told Maria that I was feeling so in love with Irene lately she said that that's how it is for alcoholics. We want what we can't have. Anyway, I'm pretty sure Maria thinks Irene's crazy from all the stories I've told her. The other day I found myself defending Irene on the phone with Maria.

Irene had only an hour before her plane took off, so we sat in the airport bar. More than anything I wanted to order a drink, but I got coffee and chain-smoked, doodling cartoons of her peasant hands on napkins. We were being silly and things felt happy, until I'd remember again our time was almost up.

"Maybe if we both save our money we can go on a road trip," I said.

"Well, we'd have to go over the summer because I just had my sabbatical, Goaty," Irene said.

"I want to go like for six months."

"Well, maybe we could go on a short one, in the meantime . . ."

"Okay, but some day I want to go on a big one where we're just gone forever, not knowing when we'll come back. Totally free."

Just me and Irene together in the car. Irene hugged me and I could smell the castile soap she used to wash her stubble with.

"Can't you stay?" I begged.

37

THE MEATLOAF IS so gross at IHOP. It's cut up into slices and then put in the freezer in little plastic-wrapped portion sizes. Someone writes the date the meatloaf was put in the freezer on a piece of masking tape. Once I looked on the tape and the meatloaf was over a year old. How disgusting!

I'm afraid of getting stuck in the freezer, so whenever I have to go in the walk-in I grab what I need and then run right out. It's an illogical fear, like when you've never stolen anything, but you get to the metal detector at the store exit and suddenly you're afraid it's going to go off, so your heart stops right as you go through the sensors. Even though I have never shoplifted in my life, I get to the detector and I freeze, thinking, what if I did put something in my bag, or what if someone else put something in my bag to frame me? I become convinced that some stranger in the store dropped something in my pocket because they want me to get arrested.

Then I think, "That's crazy! No one's going to frame me."

Or sometimes I think, "Maybe I did take something. And I don't remember taking it."

Sometimes the metal detector goes off when the clerk forgets to take the security tag off a shirt and then everyone has a real big laugh about it and says, "Well there's technology for you. Hahahahahaha, aren't we funny creatures! Ha ha ha! We can put a man on the moon but we can't let someone who has never taken a thing buy it and get out of the fucking store without the frigging alarm going off." That's how I feel when I'm in the freezer. When I first started I saw the cooks trap Molly in there as a joke and I've been petrified of them doing it to me ever since. I hate having to go in and get more salad dressing. The whole time I'm in there, I keep my eye on the big red emergency button.

* * *

I miss Irene like crazy. It took so long to stop feeling lonely after I got to San Francisco and now I feel lonely again but in a whole new way. No Jenny, no Irene, and Maria busy all the time. I went over to Molly's the other day before work, but she just spent the whole time talking about how much she hates her boyfriend's ex because I guess her boyfriend has a baby with her. I helped her fold her clean IHOP uniforms and then we walked to work together. Whenever I'm bored I just work on my book.

Even though I knew Irene was leaving, I thought it wouldn't happen if I didn't think about it. I didn't want to have to deal with saying good-bye to her like I had to say good-bye when she moved to San Francisco and I stayed down south working at Tower Records and sobbing every night.

How could Irene not know I was in love with her when I was her student at the community college? The weeks before she was getting ready to move to San Francisco I was mixed with a kind of desperation and euphoria. The source of my desperation was obvious. But the euphoria came when Irene would unexpectedly call or drop by the record store. Every extra moment I got to hang out with her staved off her leaving a tiny bit.

For a going-away present I made Irene a book. Each page described a different attribute that I found wonderful about her, without ever actually saying "I love you."

After she moved, every day on my lunch break from Tower Records I'd go to the supermarket, write a two-dollar check for potato salad, and settle myself on a bench where I'd write hourlong letters to her on yellow legal tablets that were stolen from under the register inside the store.

"Dearest Irene," I wrote. Or "Hey Divot!"—or "Wonderful Irene." "Today I ate stale marshmallow peeps that came from the back room at work." I tried to write things that would make her laugh, occasionally asking her a question or two about her life in San Francisco, but mostly rambling on about the daily events or how much I missed her. Then my hour break would be up and I'd have to go back to work. I'd stuff the letter into a stolen work envelope, affix a stolen stamp, and walk across the parking lot to drop it in the post office box.

I tried to tell Irene I was in love with her in every letter, but I could never put that into words.

What if she hates me for pretending to be her friend this whole time and never telling her my true feelings? Or, what if she thinks I'm a stupid virgin?

Eventually I admitted my love to her in writing. I finally couldn't take one more day of ignoring it. As soon as I wrote it, I looked over my shoulder to see if anyone was watching me. I worked from 3 P.M. to midnight at the record store, so my lunch break usually coincided with the sun setting. I'd scribbled I love you a thousand ways, and all of them ended up shredded into pieces and deposited at the bottom of a trash can.

"You might hate me after reading this and that's fine . . ." I'd start. Or "You are the most beautiful woman I've ever met . . ." Or "Remember when I asked you to pose naked in the cemetery for my photography assignment?"

After Irene moved I started seeing the first of many sliding-scale therapists I'd have in my life. Once I got over the initial shame of admitting my big secret of being gay to my therapist, each subsequent session was filled with tirades of my unrequited love for Irene.

"What are you afraid would happen if you told Irene you loved her?" the therapist asked me one day, exasperated with my whining.

"I could never tell her."

"But what *would happen* if you did tell her?"

She'd sounded annoyed. No wonder. She probably was annoyed listening to me whine week after week about how I could never confess my monumental love for Irene.

"There's just no way I could."

But something sank into my head after the sliding-scale therapist insisted I find the courage to share my feelings with Irene and the next day when I wrote Irene my usual letter, in the third paragraph, I confessed my love.

"There's something I've wanted to tell you for a long time but haven't had the fucking guts to do it. I love you. I'm in love with you. I love you more than I've ever loved anyone. Please don't hate me."

It took five days to get a letter back from Irene that said, "Oh Francie, I feel so foolish for not knowing. Come live with us in San Francisco. We'll dance in the ocean waves by moonlight, and live simply. Come read Audre Lorde with us over hot chocolates in the evening . . ."

I knew when Irene asked me to move to San Francisco and live simply along with Jenny and Gustavo in their little whole grain and fruit house, that she'd asked me to come not because she wanted me as her lover but because she knew I was in love with her and she felt bad excluding me.

When I first met Gustavo I saw right away what a manipulator he was. Irene said you can't blame a person for being unwell, but I feel like he uses his sickness as an excuse to hit women. Then he becomes sorry and tries to apologize, walking around dressed in all black and looking sad. Christ on a crutch. Give me a break.

He's probably beating Jenny in Seattle now. When Irene found out Jenny and Gustavo were moving to Seattle she was pissed. I'd never seen her so pissed—it was like this icy calmness. The only thing she said was, "They're obviously both in really unstable, sick places right now." She said it so compassionately and calmly it scared the shit out of me. Like maybe I'd find her in the middle of the night again ripping a phone book off a metal cable. Like that's a really stable place.

* * *

I've been having so many nightmares lately and the most depressing thing about them is that no matter what—whether I'm getting raped or stealing cars or trying to seduce some beautiful woman—I'm always waitressing, too. I never stop being a waitress.

In one dream I was on the bus in San Francisco looking for a job. I wasn't working at IHOP anymore and I was really broke. Maybe I hadn't worked in months. So I took this job as a waitress on the bus because I'd been unemployed so long. My shift was one trip around the city and I had to go up to all the people riding the bus and say, "Would you like something to drink?" but the only thing on the bus was one of those soda guns that are behind the counter at bars where you push a button, and out comes soda or seltzer. The soda gun was right next to the bus driver where you pay the fare and the only thing that came out of it was Coke. I walk up and down the aisle asking people what they wanted to drink, even though the only thing on the bus was Coke.

One lady ordered a cappuccino. When somebody wanted a cappuccino, I had to get off the bus and find the closest store that sold one, all in the time it took before the bus pulled away from the curb. In the dream it was raining, and when I went to get off the bus, a horde of people were blocking my way with their umbrellas. I knew I wouldn't be able to get the cappuccino and back on the bus again before it pulled away. I desperately wanted to quit, but the girl who trained me told me I might make fifteen dollars, and I needed the money. I got back on the bus without the cappuccino because I knew I wasn't going to make it in time. I knew I was going to get fired, but I started taking orders again, pretending that nothing was wrong. The bus lurched as it came off the electric wires, and the jolt woke me.

38

I QUIT THERAPY because Star was obsessed with talking about my childhood. Plus, a couple weeks ago I was telling her how I can't stop cutting myself even though I really want to.

"I don't think it's so bad that you cut yourself with razors," Star said casually.

At the time I didn't say anything because I was stunned. Even I know it's fucked up to cut myself with razors and I'm the least self-aware person on the planet. Besides, she was the one who made me promise to call her the next time I felt like hurting myself. I was still so pissed at her last week for saying that, I told her I didn't have any money and canceled my appointment. I was going to cancel again this week, but she left a message on my machine saying that she hoped I was okay and I'd have to pay for the appointment if I canceled again. The whole appointment I tried to tell her I felt mad about what she'd said about cutting myself, but of course I couldn't get the courage up.

After I'd spent most of the hour smoking and not saying anything, Star said, "You're quiet today. What's going on?"

The one cool thing about Star is she let me smoke in her office.

"I can't come to therapy anymore," I blurted out.

"Why not?"

"I don't have the money," I said, not looking at her.

She reached into her pocket and pulled out a pack of cigarettes, too.

"Do you mind if I smoke?"

"No, I don't care," I said, but it was a little weird to see her smoking. She took a deep drag of the cigarette and said, "Is that really why you're not coming anymore?"

"Yeah. And I also need a therapist who doesn't think it's okay that I cut myself with razors."

Star said I'd misunderstood—she wasn't saying cutting myself with razors was good. She was just saying at least I wasn't jumping off a bridge. I fidgeted in my seat.

"Okay, maybe I misunderstood you," I said, "but I still don't want to come anymore."

"Well, coming to therapy is your choice," she said. "You can call me whenever you want. Even if it's not for therapy. Like we could even grab lunch or something."

I thanked her for everything and said good-bye. Part of me felt guilty she would get a complex about being a lousy therapist since I quit and her other client killed herself. But at least now I can save my therapy money for a road trip.

* * *

Today Irene phoned me sobbing because she's really frustrated teaching her classes. I get so scared when she starts freaking out because there's nothing I can do to calm her down.

"The students aren't like you or Jenny or Gustavo. It's like they don't even care about what's going on in the world. They're not interested in nonviolence. They're just taking the class to fulfill the philosophy credit."

I was secretly happy there wasn't anyone good in her classes because when she moved back down there I was afraid she'd fall in love with some new prodigy student.

"I miss sleeping next to you," I said, trying to soothe her. "The next time you come up, I'll take such good care of you. We can go to the farmers' market and visit your friends from choir, and just be around people who care about the world."

"Hopefully, I can come up by the end of the month. I have to go to all these department meetings and start designing my new logic class."

"I really miss you," I said, trying to reassure her that she was important to me.

"Do you think I want to live down here? If I could get a job in San Francisco I would."

"Well, maybe I can come down there," I offered.

"With what money? The fifteen dollars you make a night at IHOP?"

"You don't have to say it like that."

I felt defensive.

"I'm sorry. I make so much more money than you. Of course I should be the one to come up."

I felt so depressed after I hung up the phone. Irene's mood swings were starting to make me feel like I was walking on eggshells. Maybe if I surprise her and fly down before the new semester starts it will make her feel better. That's what I'll do. I'll fly down for my birthday in August. I just have to make sure I can get the time off from IHOP.

39

I HATE HIDING when I eat at IHOP. We all have to hide when we eat. One time I snuck a short stack into the bathroom and ate it in about thirty seconds. That's one buttermilk pancake every ten seconds. I don't even think dogs can do that.

The weirdest thing anyone has ever said to me while I was waitressing was from this man who used to come in and eat buckwheat pancakes and read Tai Chi books. He said, "Never cook rice while listening to rock music, because the negative energy from the rice will lodge in your lower chakras and cause mental anguish and sexual frustration."

I said, "Oh, I was sexually frustrated and mentally anguished long before I ever listened to rock music while cooking rice."

Who were these freaks—and if they were so concerned with right livelihood and health, what were they doing eating at IHOP? I think one of my problems as a waitress is that I think I'm going to somehow make better tips if I listen to these losers, and of course the biggest freaks leave the worst tips, when they leave anything at all. I feel really at the end of my rope with IHOP. At least three times a shift, I think about throwing plates and quitting. It's just so oppressive. Julio, The Big Boss, the stupid dress. And we have to beg just to get a day off. Julio acts like the schedule is a matter of life and death—you'd think we were guarding the president.

All my poems have violent waitress rants in them now and when I try to envision what I want in my future, I can only see myself on the road with Irene. The dust swirling out from under the tires of a baby-blue Dodge Dart on a desert road.

* * *

Today I've been sober for nine months exactly. Irene called to congratulate me and say she mailed me a present.

"It's a surprise, you should get it soon."

"I've got a surprise for you, too. I'm going to come down and see you."

"Really?" she laughed and then, "Oh, you don't know how good it feels to know that I'm not the only one investing something into this relationship."

I wasn't sure exactly what she was getting at, but something about it made me feel like shit. I lit a cigarette and sat down in the Muffins Muffins chair.

"When are you coming, Goaty?"

"I'm going to ask Julio for time off today," I said. "Maybe in the next couple weeks. Maybe we can rent a car when I come down and go for a mini road trip to the desert."

"That sounds great. Call me when you know for sure when you're coming down. I love you so much."

* * *

Sometimes the only thing that stops me on my road to destruction is pounding on this typewriter—pure stream of consciousness—locked in my apartment typing. It's like talking to the most special person in the middle of the night by candlelight, sharing tea and cigarettes. I want to be able to do something with my life. I want to be a writer. I want Hope from *Days of Our Lives* to accompany me to an awards ceremony, so I could prove to my father every lesbian doesn't wear a sandwich board. Oh my god! I'm finally a published poet. I just went down to get the mail and there was a letter telling me that my poem "Pig Man, Face of Evil" is going to be published in *The Haight Ashbury Literary Journal.* I can't believe it! And I get to go to a reception and reading with the other poets in the issue.

As if that weren't enough excitement for one day, the other thing in the mailbox was this yellow padded envelope from Irene. Inside the envelope was a silver wedding band. It's just like the one I showed Irene in this jewelry store last month. On the inside of the ring she had "Ma Chèvre" engraved. That means "my goat" in French.

I'm going to run down to the AA meeting in the Mission and see if Maria's there so I can show her the ring! I called Irene three times to tell her I got her present but she wasn't home. I just hung up without leaving a message. I didn't want to seem like some ridiculous gushing teenager—I guess I feel shy. I didn't tell her about my poem being published either.

When Irene called me after she got home from work she asked if her present came.

"Oh, yeah," I said, spinning the ring on my finger. "I forgot to tell you."

I don't know why I didn't want to show her how thrilled I was she'd bought me a fucking wedding ring. I guess I still feel like I need to protect myself after everything I went through with her loving Gustavo. She told me her feelings were hurt because I wasn't more effusive. By the end of the conversation I convinced her how thrilled I was but, god, I'm such a loser for not just telling her how much I loved it in the first place.

40

MONDAY NIGHT WHEN the franchise owners came into
IHOP I was PMSing my brains out. All I could think was, "Quit
this fucking job." The franchise owner is this crazy woman who
chain-smokes, drives a Mercedes, talks on a cellular telephone, and
basically married this guy who owns seven IHOPs. Can you
imagine? An IHOP empire? The Leona Helmsley of IHOP. Anyway,
Leona Helmsley was walking around the restaurant, bossing
everyone around, telling people to wipe syrup off this and wipe
syrup off that and if I had a gun I would've shot her right there. Who
was this woman to just breeze into the restaurant in her Gucci heels
and order us to wipe the fucking syrup off everything?

So in the middle of her commanding us around, she turned and
walked down the hallway toward the bathroom and I thought, I am
going to follow her in there, wait for her to go into a stall, grab her
legs from under the door, laugh psychotically, and then quit. It was
the most lucid thought I'd ever had. It just felt so right. It's time I
went out with a bang!

I followed her down the hall, my nurse shoes squeaking the
whole way. And I was going to do it. I was going to say fuck this shit.

Fuck this bitch. Fuck this dress. Fuck this job. But then I started having second thoughts. Right about when I reached the pay phone it hit me how much I needed IHOP as a reference. I needed this job. I needed this bullshit pancake job.

Defeated, I turned around and walked back over to where Molly was putting away the clean silverware.

"Give me a steak knife," I said.

She looked at me, hesitated a moment, and then handed me a steak knife, smiling.

"If you go stab that bitch I'll give you every penny I make tonight."

As I walked back toward the bathroom I heard Molly shout, "I'm serious, Francie, every penny." I opened the door of the bathroom just as Leona Helmsley was walking out. I looked under the stall doors to make sure there were no feet and then went into the handicap stall. Slowly, I unzipped my dress and began to push the tip of the steak knife into my sternum. It was dull, not like a razor. I pushed harder into my chest to compensate for the knife's dullness. I have to be careful it doesn't go through me and pierce my lung I thought, beginning to tear at the spot near where my bra hooked in front. After I saw a little pool of blood appear, I zipped up my dress and resumed my work wiping syrup off things.

* * *

Julio twitched nervously and made farting noises as he moved his weight back and forth on the vinyl booth, trying to settle into a comfortable position. He and The Big Boss were discussing whether I could take the time off that I'd asked for to go see Irene.

"Francie, you can't take vacation in August," Julio said.

"Why?"

"We're very busy in August. I need you to take a vacation in October. There aren't as many tourists in San Francisco then."

"But I already got my plane ticket, Julio."

"I need you to go in October or the first few weeks of November. That's a good time to go."

"Jul-i-o. I bought my ticket already. I can't return it. I need the first week of August off."

"Sorry, Francie."

"Okay. That's fine, I'll just quit if you can't give me the time off, Julio." It wasn't a threat. It was exactly what I would do.

He shifted his weight again in the vinyl booth, momentarily lifting his darty eyes to meet mine. I leaned back, stretching my legs across my side of the booth. Anxiety began bubbling inside me.

The Big Boss, who hadn't said a thing, got up because he saw his chicken appear under the heat lamp in the kitchen window. I took a cigarette out of my pack and lit it.

"You are doing so good, Francie. You've got an apartment now. You're not a hostess, you're a waitress," Julio said, pumping me up about the benefits of IHOP.

He continued to talk about how he thought IHOP had improved my life. It all came down to: before I was living with people and now I could afford my own apartment.

"Julio, if you won't give me time off in August or you can't, that's fine, I'll just quit. I told you, I have no problem quitting."

At this point The Big Boss came back with his chicken, cigarette hanging out of his mouth. IHOP employees were making the shift change between breakfast and dinner around us. It was Sunday. The late-afternoon light leaked in the windows. The Big Boss paused for a second, set his plate of chicken down, and glared at my legs stretched out on the booth.

"Get your goddamned feet off my goddamned booth," he said, swiping at my nurse shoes with his hand.

"What did you say to me?" I asked very quietly.

"I told you to get your goddamned feet off my goddamned booth."

My hands reached around the back of me, feeling for the ties of my apron. Fingers dug into my pockets and grabbed my pen and book of checks. Click, click, click—I heard the sound of my grease pen skipping across the tile floor.

"Fuck this fucking place. I fucking quit," I said, marching to the locker room.

I pulled my crumpled knapsack out of the locker and lit a cigarette. Next, I unzipped my dress and pulled out my sweatpants. Normally, when I took off my ninety-nine-cent nude stockings, I did so trying to preserve them for one more shift. Now that I knew I'd never need them again, I happily ripped them off. On my way out of IHOP, I walked past The Big Boss and Julio. They sat exactly where I'd left them moments before when I'd bolted upright and thrown my pen. They said nothing as I walked out—confirming what I already felt in the changing room: I was finally done at IHOP.

Outside it was typically San Francisco. The wind blew hard under an apocalyptically bright sun. As always I walked the exact route of the bus—that way if it did come up the street I'd be able to decide whether or not I was tired enough to get on. My legs moved fast. I felt the same way inside as the one time I ran away from home. Excited, but scared. I was afraid to be okay with quitting. The days had turned into weeks and the weeks into month and now nine months later I was changed. From virgin to someone who had more than one lover. Woman lovers. I'd fallen in love, had two bad therapists, and learned to carry many plates on one arm.

I wanted my mother. To be small. First grade, sitting on the bench at the mall across from Hot Dog on a Stick. I stared at my liberated face in the plastic pane of the newspaper stand. I smiled at myself. Where was I going? I was going home to call Irene and tell her I had quit. I was going to shave the sides of my head and make sure IHOP would never take me back. My cheeks and the tops of my ears burned from the cold and it was almost August.

Irene and I will leave town together and go on a road trip. No one will stop us. She is the love of my life. I'll bounce up and down on her hand in a motel room, then curl up and eat pizza and fall asleep. At the corner of Geary and Polk Street I sucked down the last bit of my cigarette and tossed it into the gutter. My lungs burned from walking so fast and smoking.

I sat down next to Andy on his cardboard box and told him that I quit my job. I wished Irene was upstairs in my apartment so we could go celebrate my quitting with a hamburger at the Tumbleweed.

"Guess what," I told Andy, "I just quit my job."

"Did you make a real big scene when you quit?" he asked wide-eyed.

"I wish."

I think a serious, "How am I living up to my anarchist potential?" assessment is necessary when I quit a job in the future.

41

I GAVE MYSELF a mohawk! Now even if Julio calls and begs me to come back to IHOP, he won't be able to hire me because my hair is against IHOP regulations. It has been a week since I quit, and this is the first time I've even felt halfway motivated to write any kind of exposé about it.

I feel like going into IHOP and acting like a mental patient. Although I guess there were a lot of customers that were like that who didn't piss off anyone. Corporate bullshit. I think it would be fair to say that franchises are evil. Everything is evil. Everything is evil. Everything is evil. Everything is evil. Everything is evil. It gives me great satisfaction to type that phrase over and over as fast as I can. Like some kind of sex. Not out of love or seduction or power, just quick sex to get the toxic buzzing out of your system. Although I don't think I am nearly done processing this nine-month relationship with IHOP. *Nobody does breakfast like IHOP! Or lunch! Or dinner!* That's the annoying slogan that's printed 6,000 times all over the paper placemats. That fucking annoying exclamation point! It's like who are you trying to convince?

42

I'D NEVER TOLD anyone about the money I'd hidden in the wall. Once when I was in bed with Jenny, I'd gotten the urge to tell her we could buy a cheap car and take off together. The night I quit IHOP, I'd thought about sawing open the wall to see how much was in there. I hadn't been out of work two hours and I already started freaking out about paying my bills and losing my apartment. If I can just know how much money is in the wall, then I'll know how soon I need to get a job. But I was afraid without a plan, I'd piddle away my money eating hamburgers at the Tumbleweed Café.

When I'd first told Irene I'd quit IHOP, I was hysterical—not hysterical crying, but giddy and chain-smoking and cussing.

"They didn't want me to take a fucking vacation in August. I mean can you believe that? Fucking Julio. I told him I'd already bought my plane ticket and he didn't even care. I should burn my dresses!" I said. "I feel like taking my uniforms down to that alley next to the Polk Gulch where people burn shit, and just watch them go up in smoke."

Irene was quiet for a while, and then she said, "What are you going to do for money? You're going to need another job if you want to keep your apartment."

"I don't know what I'm going to do yet. I guess I'm going to see how much money I have saved. Maybe I'll go on a road trip."

"Go on a road trip, without me?" Irene said.

As soon as she said it, I felt afraid of the panicked tone of her voice.

"Not without you. I mean, maybe I'll just travel around until you get a break from school and then you can come meet me."

"You need to get a car and you'll need money for motels and food. All that stuff costs a lot of money."

"Well, maybe I can get a job until you can come, too," I offered.

"I don't think you understand. I just came off a sabbatical that I took after being at the college for only one year. It's not like I can just leave again whenever I want. This is a tenure-track position. Do you understand what that means?"

"Yes," I said. But I didn't really understand.

* * *

I borrowed a saw from the guy at the liquor store downstairs and cut a hole in the wall of my apartment. It was a lot harder than I thought it would be and there was white dust everywhere, all caught in my nose hairs. For a second I was afraid I was breathing in asbestos. I reached my hand in the hole and kept ripping bigger and bigger pieces of drywall away until I was staring at a giant gaping hole. Inside the wall were close to two hundred plastic sandwich bags filled with money. It was amazing. I almost started crying because it felt like I'd found a treasure chest. Then I scooped out all the plastic bags with tips in them, and guess what? After separating everything into stacks and recounting three times I have $4,798.43. Almost $5,000. Isn't that crazy? I had to go downstairs to get a pack of cigarettes and a Coke just to be able to deal with the fact that there was so much money in my wall.

"Guess how much money I have?" I said when Irene called.

"How much?"

"Almost five thousand dollars."

"What!"

"Isn't that crazy? It was all in the wall."

"In the wall??"

"Oh, yeah. I was saving money in this hole in the wall. The girls at work told me about it. That way you can't take it out and spend it."

"How did you get it in the wall?"

"I had this hole that I dropped it in behind that picture of you lying next to the tombstone in the cemetery?"

"What kind of secret double life are you leading?" Irene joked, "I can't believe you were hiding money in your wall and you didn't even tell me. Did you have to blow the whole wall up to get the money out?"

"Pretty much. I cut this huge hole. It was amazing—the wall was filled with plastic bags of cash. I need to fix it before Bill sees."

"You had five thousand dollars in cash in the wall of your apartment?" Irene asked again incredulously.

"We could buy a car and then take off. Nothing is stopping us. After our trip you could get another job. Anyone would hire you. You're a total genius."

"If I could get a job 'anywhere,' then I wouldn't be freaking out. I can't get a job just anywhere, Goaty."

Her voice started to bristle.

"Run away with me, Irene. You hate living down there anyway and no one in your classes gets what you're really trying to tell them about nonviolence and peace. We could live so simply."

"You hate living simply. You couldn't even go one Wednesday without white flour."

"I know. But I'm different now. I feel like I'm ready to challenge myself to live a more healthy, nonviolent life."

I could hear her start to cry on the other end of the phone.

"What's the matter? Aren't you happy?"

"I can't believe you're telling me all this when I don't live there anymore. You never wanted to be a part of Simplicity House. How am I supposed to believe things are different now? You say a million different things. You said you loved me, and then you slept with Jenny. How do I know what's the truth?"

"Don't cry. It's just now that you're gone, I know more than ever how much I need to be with you."

"Well, it's too late now, Goaty. You should've told me you wanted to go on a road trip before I made the decision to come back from my sabbatical. I can't just pick up and go now."

"Okay. We'll figure something out. I'll do anything it takes to be with you."

After I hung the phone up with Irene, I was filled with guilt for all the time I fucked around with Jenny when I first moved to San Francisco. Even though Irene was wrapped up with Gustavo and the craziness of Simplicity House, I wished I could've somehow just swallowed my pain while waiting for her instead of creating my own drama. Hearing her voice on the phone made me realize that I'd never loved anyone more than her. No wonder I'd followed her to San Francisco.

* * *

Today I brought Maria flowers at the gay AA meeting. I pretended they were for her AA anniversary but really I just wanted to hand her a huge bouquet in front of everyone. I still feel my blood race when I stare at her beautiful, long legs. I know it's fucked up to give Maria flowers after Irene bought me a ring, but what can I do? I love women! At the meeting I sat behind Maria and the whole time I wanted to tap her on the shoulder and ask her if I could braid her hair. Finally, I got up the courage to do it.

"Can I braid your hair?"

"Shhh." She smiled. "Pay attention."

Even though she was smiling when she said it, I felt a little rejected.

"Oh, okay," I said, immediately starting to braid a strand of my mohawk. I tried to play it off as my insatiable desire to braid as opposed to the fact that I wanted to touch Maria. But I don't know if she even saw me braiding my hair because I was sitting behind her. Plus, I'm constantly playing with my hair. The mohawk is pretty long now. Sometimes I rub the stubble on the side of my head and it makes me feel like I'm petting Irene.

* * *

Today William came over and helped me fix the wall. It looks like new. He was really impressed at how good I was at hanging drywall.

"I used to work for this guy in AA who was a handyman," I said. "I learned it all from him."

It was nice to see William.

"How's IHOP?"

"What do you think, Francie? Everyone's so jealous you got out."

He tried to convince me to drive with him to Reno so he could gamble all night but instead we just walked around the Castro smoking and talking before we ended up at Sparky's.

"I want to go on a road trip," I told him. "I'm going to look at a Ford Falcon van tomorrow.

"That sounds so great, just being on the road and not having to be anywhere at any time."

"I know."

"Are you going alone?"

For a second I thought he was going to ask if he could come with me. And I didn't know how I would tell him no.

"I want Irene to come, but I don't know if she can. She has this good job. She's a professor."

"Wow. You banged your professor. That's hot."

"William, shut up," I said, smiling and stealing a cigarette from his pack.

When I got home that night there was a message on my answering machine from Irene. Her voice had this really comatose shutdown tone. I was scared she tried to kill herself and imagined her dead a million different ways. Luckily, she answered when I called.

"What's up?" I asked, trying to sound chipper.

"Gustavo called me freaked out to tell me he got Jenny pregnant."

"What!"

"I can't believe this. Gustavo knows he's not ready to be a father."

"Is she going to have an abortion?"

"I don't know. He asked me if they should get married."

"Oh my god. He's crazy, Irene. Jenny needs to get out of there."

"When we were together he swore he never wanted kids. He was my lover. Now he seems like a stranger."

I felt a tinge of rage listening to Irene, who seemed oblivious that what she was saying might make me jealous.

"I'm so sick of everyone lying to me. And abandoning me. I think I have all these important things in my life and they just disappear. Simplicity House. Jenny. Gustavo. No one cares about nonviolence. My teaching isn't changing anyone's thinking about the world."

"You're the best teacher I ever had," I said, trying to reassure.

"I have no idea what the Goddess wants me to be doing."

"I'm still planning on coming down to visit."

"Why? So we can sit in this oppressive tract home? I don't want you here. I want to be with you there. I need to be in San Francisco. To see you. But I can't right now. I need some time to think about what I'm doing with my life."

It was hours later when we hung up the phone and I was depressed from another one of Irene's inconsolable mood swings. Her level of hopelessness scares the shit out of me.

43

A WEEK AFTER Irene had called to tell me Jenny was pregnant with Gustavo's baby, she flew up at the last minute to surprise me for the weekend. I borrowed William's truck and picked her up at the airport.

"Hi," I said, giving her a giant hug.

"Hi," she said, holding on to me tightly. What was it about being in her arms that always made everything okay?

"I've got to return William's truck before seven, so why don't I drop you off at my apartment and you can take a bath and relax. I'll pick us up something to eat. We can get a pizza and stay in for the night."

"I want vegetables," she moaned. "I'll just go to the produce stand on the corner."

By the time I'd gotten back from dropping the truck off, Irene was in the kitchen trying to make a stir-fry.

"You don't have anything to cook with. How do you eat? *What* do you eat?"

"Top Ramen and toast."

I hugged her from behind as she stirred the vegetables in my fucked-up frying pan that I'd bought for a quarter at the Salvation Army.

I ate a little bit of the vegetables, but mostly I was disappointed we weren't at the Tumbleweed Café.

After dinner Irene examined the patched-up wall.

"There was five thousand dollars in there?" she asked again.

"Yeah. Can you believe I managed to save that much money?"

"See what a person can do if they live off one pack of Top Ramen a week," Irene joked.

Her mood seemed to be lightening so I didn't ask her anything about work, or Gustavo and Jenny. We made out a tiny bit and cuddled, but we didn't have sex. Irene was exhausted because she'd barely slept since Gustavo told her Jenny was pregnant. I lay next to her and listened to her snore. Eventually, I drifted off, too. In the middle of the night her panicked crying woke me.

"It's okay," I said, "it's just a dream."

"Every night I have teaching nightmares—no one's listening, the chalk keeps breaking on the chalkboard . . ."

I put my hand on her sweaty forehead.

"I've been wanting to tell you something," Irene started.

I braced myself for the worst. Was she leaving me for Gustavo? Was Jenny going to have an abortion because Gustavo still wanted to be with Irene?

"It's why I came up here this weekend. I wanted to tell you in person."

"You're making me nervous."

"I gave notice at the college."

"What?"

"I don't know what the Goddess wants for me, but I know I'm not supposed to be teaching right now."

"But you just started there again," I said, feeling scared she was making such a huge decision. "You always said you were so lucky for getting a tenure-track job so young in life."

"I'm sick of traveling back and forth to see you and it's only just started. Do you know how stressful it is to be at the airport so much,

and not have a home of my own? I'm leaving my whole life—
everything I have worked for up to now, I'm leaving it behind. I'm
willing to do it if it means getting to be with you."

"Irene, I don't want you to quit your job just to be with me."

"But every day you call me and tell me how much you want me
to move here so we can live together. You write me letters and post-
cards saying how you long for the day when just the two of us can
be on the open road."

"Yeah," I said, "but I didn't mean quit your job *for me*. I only
wanted you to quit if *you wanted* to."

"What are you saying?"

"I just don't want to be responsible for you quitting your job."

"The whole point of being lovers with someone is to be responsible to each other, Goaty. To make sacrifices for the good of the
relationship."

Her voice was starting to quaver again. I didn't say anything.

"I didn't fly up here because I was upset about Gustavo and Jenny.
I wanted to tell you I gave my notice at the college a few days ago. "

"But it all seems so sudden."

"My life is not in Southern California anymore. I know I'm
being called to San Francisco, for a variety of reasons," Irene said.

"But if we go on a road trip we're not going to be in San Francisco," I reminded Irene. I was afraid to even mention the road trip,
but I wasn't sure what she was getting at. I worried she'd see it as
another demand for her to sacrifice something. "I already started
looking at cars to buy this week," I said. "I can't believe we actually
might be going." I kissed her deeply.

"Goaty, I never planned on falling in love with you. You surprised me. But we're partners now. You're the one who takes care of
me and who I take care of. We're each other's and I couldn't think of
anything more magnificent than going on the road with you."

"Really?"

"Yeah," Irene said, smiling.

The apartment was still dark, but I wanted to get up right then and start looking at classifieds for used cars.

"I have to finish teaching the summer session. The soonest I could be ready to go would be in two weeks," Irene said.

"That's so long!"

Irene flashed me a look of anger.

"Just kidding," I said, "that will give me time to find a car and get everything we need. Is the college mad at you?"

"They're not mad. It's just a hassle for them to get someone this quickly before the fall semester. I was too radical for them anyway. When they denied my course proposal to teach Philosophy of Non-violence again, that sealed the deal for me. I just thought I'm not going to waste my life teaching Logic and Intro to Philosophy."

"When do you have to go back?"

"Tomorrow," Irene said. Then she looked out the window and saw the early-morning light. "I mean, today."

"But you just got here."

"This is the last time we have to part from each other. After this we'll be together for good."

44

WILLIAM IS GOING to sublet my apartment while I'm on my road trip. That way I won't have to give it up, and after we get back Irene and I can decide whether we want to live together or not. I don't think Irene wants to live with me in my apartment, though, because she thinks it's too small for the both of us.

William offered us the use of his truck, too. He's wanted to sell it lately anyway because it's too much of a pain in the ass to have a truck in San Francisco, but he can't bear to part with it because he's had it for so long. But in the last two months he's gotten over five hundred dollars in parking tickets and he said if I pay for them and a new clutch, then I can use it for as long as I want. I hope it doesn't break down—but if it does it will be an even bigger adventure. The great thing is we can sleep in the back if we want so we won't need to pay for motels. And the more money we save on things, the longer we can be away.

* * *

Irene got here this morning. I can't believe we're finally going to be together! Just her and me. In the same city, never having to be apart again!

I felt really sad saying good-bye to Maria and my apartment. It even felt sad saying good-bye to William.

"Be careful," he said. "I'll take good care of your place."

I covered my typewriter with a small dish towel and pushed it to the side of the table so it would be out of William's way. It looked so nice sitting there in the sun. If I had one of those travel typewriters that didn't need electricity I could bring that on the trip. But I'm going to have to do all my writing on paper.

Irene wanted to drive first. She said it made her feel free. The first thing I did once we got on the freeway was light a cigarette. Irene said, "You're not going to smoke in the truck the whole time, are you?" But it just seems right that you should smoke on a road trip and hang your hand out the window.

We were only an hour north of San Francisco when I began my first letter to Maria.

Irene said, "You're writing letters already, and we've only been gone an hour?"

But it was so hard to say good-bye to Maria this morning. I wish she could've come with us. I bet she wouldn't hassle me about smoking in the truck.

I asked Irene if our first stop could be Provo, Utah, where my old high school friend Michelle lives. At first she didn't seem into it because it was north and we were planning on going south.

"We're not in a rush," I said, "we have six months."

Irene reluctantly agreed, so I called Michelle from a pay phone and told her to ask her boss for a few days off so she could go camping with us.

"How long are you traveling for?" she said.

"Six months."

And then I immediately felt panicky at the thought of being away from home for six months. I was missing my typewriter and my apartment already. I guess I never realized how much time I spent by myself in my apartment writing and how happy it made me. It's not like I'm depressed. I just feel weird not being able to be alone to do my writing.

Michelle and Irene immediately hit it off and I was so happy. I'd told Michelle so much about Irene in letters that I was glad she was finally getting a chance to meet her. I let them sit together in the front seat and I sprawled out in the back of the truck, watching the scenery speed by. By early evening we found a campsite and set up camp. Some girls from another campsite came over and invited us to a bonfire at their campsite. I couldn't figure out if they were gay.

"We're just going to hang out by the fire. We shoplifted some beer and chocolate from the general store," they said.

I simultaneously worshipped and was scared of them. A really young blond girl kept passing the beer back to Irene. I wasn't used to seeing Irene drink. She'd told me she used to drink a lot in college, but I'd never seen her drink much at all. Since I was the only one at the bonfire not drinking, I fixated on Irene. She took big, giant, tough swigs of beer like she was in a movie. She was so sexy when she looked tough. I crawled next to her and bit her neck in front of the blond girl, just in case she had any ideas about stealing Irene. I really wanted to drink with everyone else. It seemed like fun getting trashed and roasting marshmallows.

After a little while I slipped away and called Maria from the pay phone at the general store. She didn't answer so I left her a message telling her how badly I wanted to drink. After I hung up, I realized she was going to worry about me drinking but have no way to get in touch with me. I hadn't thought about that. I quickly justified my worrying her by telling myself she was probably fucking Ashanti and that's why she didn't answer the phone.

The morning after the bonfire I went with Irene and Michelle for a hike in the canyon. During the hike, Irene kept asking me what was wrong because I was quiet.

"I feel a little depressed," I said. "It's weird to not be working on my writing."

Was that true? I know I'd gotten jealous at the pay phone thinking about Maria fucking Ashanti. Something about it filled me with a terrible longing. Like I wanted to be the one that took Maria on dates and wooed her. Or I wanted to be excited about Irene like when I first met her. It used to be I got weak looking at her no matter what. Plus Irene isn't sophisticated like Maria. Maria reminds me of Hope from *Days of Our Lives,* with all that long dark hair. Irene's some other kind of femme with her shaved head.

After the hike we packed up the camp because we needed to get Michelle back in time for work. On the way out of the campground we saw the girls from the bonfire and waved good-bye to them. Irene gave them my address in San Francisco.

"We'll probably be gone for six months," she said, telling the blond one, in case she wrote before we got back, she'd know someone was collecting my mail.

Who were these girls and why did Irene give them my address? What kind of letter could they possibly write us after only hanging out once with us at a campfire? I worried for a second that something might've happened with Irene and the blond girl when I left the bonfire to call Maria from the pay phone. Later I'd have to ask Michelle if anything happened with Irene and the blond girl. I tried to doze in the back of the truck while they sat in the front on the way back to Provo. Irene must think Michelle's cool because this time she didn't complain about having to drive so far out of the way to get Michelle home.

* * *

Don't believe the hype about the Grand Canyon—it isn't what it's cracked up to be. After seeing Canyonlands and Zion National Park and having driven through the Painted Desert, the Grand Canyon just didn't seem like a big deal. Irene was really interested in reading from the guidebook about the people in the park that die every year.

Either they hiked to the bottom of the canyon and forgot to bring water or they disrupted a sleeping rattlesnake. How could you hike to the bottom of the canyon and not bring water? Jesus Christ. The reasons for death were fairly varied, although I'd never sat down and really thought about all the ways a person could die at the Grand Canyon.

My father loves survivalist stories—lost hikers who have to cut their own legs off with a penknife after becoming trapped beneath an errant boulder.

"Imagine cutting your own leg off with a penknife. And then, as if that wasn't enough, having to climb three miles out, on one leg. Then getting back to your car, but the car is a stick shift. The guy had to drive himself to the hospital, the whole time shifting with one leg."

My father could tell that story a thousand times. The only difference between the stories my father likes and the stories Irene was reading me from the guidebook were people sometimes survived in my father's stories.

The stories in the guidebook, on the other hand, were a cautionary tale.

Irene and I had tried to find an unpopulated area to set up our tent, but the Grand Canyon's filled with tourists, unlike some of the less-traveled parks we'd been to. We ended up finding a campsite close to the rim of the canyon. After the tent was set up, we climbed inside. Despite the sun beating down through the tent, I felt sleepy, and oddly chilly. Irene laughed when I crawled inside the sleeping bag to warm up.

"It's eighty degrees out," she said.

"I know, but the wind feels cold."

I realized this was the first time since we'd left on our trip that Irene and I were alone in the tent together. She crawled into my sleeping bag and we made out a little.

"I don't know why I'm so tired," I said.

"Are you trying to get out of kissing me?" Irene teased.

"No, I feel like someone drugged me."

"Come on," she said standing up. "Let's go look at the Grand Canyon. It'll wake you up to go for a walk."

I couldn't imagine anything worse than going for a walk around the Grand Canyon at that moment but I didn't know how to get out of it. I grabbed my camera and we laced up our shoes outside the tent. While Irene prepared Grey Poupon and vegetable sandwiches, I wandered around our campsite looking for things to take pictures of. I looked at the red rock canyon and tried to imagine Evel Knievel jumping across it on his motorcycle. Then my boot ran into a piece of eaten corn on the cob that was lying in the parking lot. Irene walked toward me with a whole sandwich for me in one hand and her almost finished one in the other.

"I kept calling you to tell you the sandwiches were ready. What are you doing?"

"I'm making art," I said, snapping a picture of the corn.

She laughed when she realized what I was taking a picture of and situated one of her sandals next to the corncob.

"Now take a picture," she said.

We took pictures of the corncob at all different angles, with and without Irene's sandals. Then Irene held the corncob like a microphone and sang into it. She scratched her chin pensively, holding the corncob as a pencil. The corncob as a young poet. We were fixated. I forgot how fun Irene could be when she was silly. It felt good to laugh.

At first finding the corncob had been fun, but the more we wandered, the more litter we discovered. For a national park, the Grand Canyon was really messy. Irene got more and more irritated by each new discovery of trash.

"I don't know why people can't manage to pick up their trash, especially when visiting a national park," Irene shouted to no one in particular after she accidentally kicked a dirty diaper with her sandal.

And then later when we walked through what looked like a fraternity party campsite, "Pick up your trash! You're in a national park!"

I thought we were going to get our asses kicked big time, but mostly people just stared. We found a somewhat secluded scenic lookout and stared out across the canyon. Irene stood behind me with her arms wrapped around my waist.

"So what do you think about the Grand Canyon?" Irene whispered.

I tried to make myself feel something as I looked at the sun setting on the other side of the red canyon, but I couldn't. It looked exactly like a postcard. I felt like I was in the postcard. The depressed young lesbian standing in the shadow of a cactus.

"To tell you the truth—I don't really see what the big deal is," I said.

We decided to leave the next day because there were so many people everywhere, it was a tourist hell. I packed up the tent while Irene cleaned the pots and pans and put out the fire. We'd had gritty cowboy coffee that was bitter and left my teeth filled with grounds. As we drove out of the campsite, Irene yelled, "litterer," out the window at a frat boy who was dumping some beer cans into the bushes. Then she sped away before he could throw anything at us.

"I'm so fucking tired," I said.

"Should we go to the doctor?"

"No, I'm just going to close my eyes while you drive."

We drove a little farther, the traffic heavy on the main route leaving the park. Every time Irene tapped the brake and shifted back into first gear I woke from my nap. A hitchhiker was walking up the side of the road with a sign that said, "Disneyland or Bust." He looked about twenty-two with long stringy hippie hair.

Irene stuck her head out the window and said, "We're not going to Disneyland, but do you want a ride down to the main highway?"

He didn't even answer, just picked up his hippie backpack and scrambled into the back of the truck. Irene opened the window that separated the cab from its shell. I closed my eyes and pretended to sleep. His filthy hippie smell drifted in the window.

"Thanks for picking me up, sister," he said in his stoned little voice.

Immediately he reminded me of Gustavo with his pretense of earnestness. Irene made small talk. I was worried that he'd change his mind and want to drive all the way to Phoenix with us. The nicer Irene was to him, the more I worried, but thankfully he scrambled out at the entrance to the park, hoping to catch someone heading to California.

"Why are you going to Disneyland?" Irene had asked when he first got in.

"It's like the happiest place on earth, right?" he sung in his stoned little voice.

I found him so enraging I wanted to blurt out, "Walt Disney was an alcoholic wife beater. How's that for happy?"

After we dropped him off, I watched him put on his headphones and begin to dance, twirling his entire body in giant circles. I hoped he'd end up as another Grand Canyon casualty—dancing himself into a state of fatal dehydration.

* * *

We drove late into the night because we were looking for a good campsite but the only one we could find was gross and full of weeds. It wasn't until we'd set up the tent that we realized the site had no shower or bathroom facility. In fact, it seemed more like a disgusting field on the side of the road with a few BBQ pits than a campsite. I was sure this would be the campsite where we got murdered for being lesbians. It was a few hundred feet up the road from a liquor and ammo store. I've never understood how it was legal for liquor and ammunition to legally coexist in the same store.

I set up the tent while Irene made a fire. There were only a few other campers at the campsite, but thankfully no one was right next to us. Sitting in front of the fire, Irene rubbed my back sweetly, but I was getting eaten alive by mosquitoes.

"Fucking shit," I said after getting bit for the fiftieth time. "I can't sit out here anymore."

I was beginning to feel more and more depressed. I tried to lie down in the tent, but there was no way to get comfortable. It felt like I was lying in a field of rocks, which I was. Irene kept crawling out of the tent to try and brush the rocks out of the way. Then she'd lie back down, find a rock under her shoulder blade, and repeat the whole process on the other side of the tent. I felt useless being unable to help her, but I was too depressed to move.

While Irene struggled with the rocks, I listened for someone to sneak up out of the brush and kill us. Finally, Irene crawled back inside, her hands smelling like dirt. She was strangely cheery and amorous, kissing me, but it made me feel claustrophobic. I tried to force myself to look at her and want sex, but I could only smell our dirty feet mixed with the plastic of the tent. I finally understood what people meant when they said sex can become a chore.

For the first time in weeks I felt like cutting myself. Suddenly, everything was wrong with Irene. Everything that had been right for so long, perfect, had become undesirable. Irene was getting turned on kissing me, and I floated above my body, thinking about all the other people I'd rather be making out with. I could tell she wanted me to fuck her. We still hadn't had sex on the trip and it had been days.

"Touch me," she said.

My heart sank.

"I'd rather watch you touch yourself," I lied.

I'd said it in the same way we'd said it to each other before, in my best sexy voice. Once those words had been a turn-on. But saying them now made me incredibly sad.

"I don't want to touch myself. I want you to touch me."

I tried to force myself to move, but I couldn't. Irene's realization of my disinterest registered in her and she burst into hard, short sobs.

"Why do all my lovers stop wanting me?" she cried.

"I still want you," I said, holding her awkwardly. "I'm just feeling really depressed for some reason. It's me, not you."

It was useless to try and comfort Irene. I didn't even have the energy to try and tell convincing lies. What was happening to me? Why didn't I want to have sex?

* * *

The next day we drove in silence to a commune Irene had heard about that made wind chimes and ceramic pots. From the road, the modern, solar dormitories gave it a cult-like feeling.

"There's a tour that starts in an hour. We can get some coffee at the café while we wait."

"That sounds great," I said, dreading the thought of having to be here for ten minutes, let alone a few hours.

At the café Irene read about the commune. People apply for two-year internships where they either learn ceramics or wind chime assembly. The items are then sold, and after the commune's expenses are covered, profits are donated to various local charities. Interns sleep in dorms and live for "free," if you count eating gruel and assembling wind chimes for eight hours a day as free.

"This sounds amazing," Irene said.

It scared me to think she would so quickly think about living in some commune with strangers.

The tour seemed to last forever. Michael was our tour guide and resident sculptor. He had a long dark ponytail down his back and wore Jesus sandals. His hands and clothes were covered in plaster dust. Irene kept asking questions and making jokes with him when we walked from one station to the next. I lingered a few steps behind. We saw the sculpture area, the kitchen, a community garden. There were about ten people on the tour, and everyone but me seemed spellbound. Irene was shamelessly flirting with Michael. I wondered if she was trying to get back at me for not wanting to have sex last night. My impotence wasn't going to stop her from being a sexual creature. Michael ended the tour by showing us the completely solar-powered dormitories where interns slept.

The tour group started to disperse and Irene cornered Michael.

"I'm definitely considering applying. This is exactly the kind of community I've always wanted to be a part of."

"You should definitely apply," he encouraged.

I tried to watch his eyes to see if he was shooting her any meaningful looks. Was she really considering this? I felt simultaneously scared and relieved at the thought of losing Irene to the wind-chime cult.

Walking back to the truck in the parking lot she seemed genuinely happy. Why did she always need an earnest hippie dude to put her in a good mood? Still, I was relieved to have her not sobbing.

I decided to drive for a change. I was bored just looking out the window and worrying about why I finally had what I'd wanted for so long but felt unhappy. As soon as we were in the truck Irene said, "I feel like I could do the Goddess's work here."

"Making wind chimes," I joked. I instantly felt mean when I heard my own voice but Irene didn't seem to notice.

"I need to live simply again. Communally."

"I told you I'd live simply with you," I said. Suddenly the thought of losing Irene terrified me.

"We're life partners, Goaty, but I still want to live and work with others. I got a really good feeling from Michael. He seemed committed to working for equality."

"I'm sure he's a great person," I said.

* * *

I drove in the direction of a deer petting zoo I'd seen signs for. How exciting to be in a place filled with deer you could touch. I turned the radio up and imagined kissing the deer. They'll gather around me and we'll lie down together under the shade of a tree. I'll rest my face against their beautiful skulls covered in short auburn bristles. And we'll kiss. My mouth on the deer mouth—romantically, not filled with lust. This wouldn't be slipping into the pasture at night and having my way with a sheep. It never occurred to me before, how much I loved deer. I smiled thinking about it.

"You're suddenly in a good mood," Irene said.

"I'm so excited to go here," I said pulling into the parking lot.

We entered the office of the deer petting zoo. A lady sat behind the counter, selling cracked corn and pellets in paper cups for a dollar.

"We get to feed them, too," I hollered excitedly. "Oh my god. You're so lucky to work here," I told the lady.

"How many cups do you want?" she remarked bitterly.

"Is there a limit? I don't want them to get sick from eating too much."

"There's no limit."

Her indifference diluted my excitement a tad. I was so tired of humans and their emotions. I bought five cups of feed, but Irene only wanted one.

We walked through the back door of the office into the dirt compound. I was grateful I knew how to waitress because it wasn't easy to maneuver all the paper cups filled with feed. I decided that with the exception of one cup, I'd pour the feed into my pockets so my hands would be free to pet the deer. The deer immediately galloped toward us.

"Look at all of them coming over here. They sense we're their friends," I told Irene, sticking my hand out to touch the head of a small, spotted female. It bypassed me completely, as I tried to cop a feel. Then I tried to touch another, and it, too, cowered while others lunged at the paper cup. I learned quickly the only way for me to touch the deer was to pour corn in the palm of one hand and swiftly rub the head of whatever deer came to devour it. The deer soon realized I had some food in my pocket and we began to do a dance. When they leaned forward to sniff my pocket, I tried to touch them before they darted away. It broke my heart to see them run away from me skittishly. They were treating me like a perpetrator.

Where was the meadow filled with shy fawns waiting solely to meet me? Instead, the deer were mangy and piss-soaked, pushing their faces at me greedily. I managed to touch a few bristly heads, but mostly they succeeded in escaping my advances.

"Stay still. I want to touch you," I said, running after a terrified little Bambi who I managed to corner between a tree and the wall. I reached for a patch of tiny white spots on its ass. "Don't be afraid, I just want to touch you," I repeated.

"Touch yourself," Bambi answered before slipping out of the corner.

Irene had no interest in touching the deer. She was content to be Mother Teresa, scattering the corn on the ground humbly. Why didn't she need the deer to fight to the death over who got to kiss her? Why didn't she need the proof of desire as she watched the deer pull each other limb from limb, competing for her love?

The one Napoleon deer who managed to get most of the food by menacing the rest away began to gnaw at my empty jeans pocket where I'd first poured the corn. I looked at his big yellow teeth gnaw at my thigh. Then a few others came to nip at my forearms and the backs of my knees. I'd let them fight over me. At first the quick nipping hurt, but then I smiled as the little bites sent pain radiating through the rest of my body.

Irene wandered over to me.

"Do you know they're biting you?" she asked incredulously.

I gave her a big opium-den smile.

"God. Aren't they beautiful? Don't you want to kiss them?" I asked.

"No."

"Fuck. I do. I'd do anything to kiss them on the mouth."

*　*　*

I was high off the deer petting zoo for hours. Irene seemed really unchanged from the experience and it added to me feeling far away from her. I couldn't get over the fact that she wouldn't kiss the deer on the mouth if she had the chance.

We camped about a hundred miles from Santa Fe and in the morning Irene bought me some loose tobacco and a corncob pipe from the gas station. I tried to smoke out of it but I could only taste the plastic. She decided to go on a small hike and I was grateful for a chance alone to write in my journal. I opened my journal up on the picnic table and sat for a second, trying to find a place to start. I was hollow like a bird bone. I missed sitting at my typewriter and looking out onto the fire escape.

I tried to write Irene a love poem. It had once been so easy, but now whenever I tried to fantasize about kissing her I could only think of kissing Maria. How come when I thought of being Maria's girlfriend I felt alive, but when I thought about being with Irene I felt trapped? I finally had the woman I'd said I do anything to be with. She'd quit her job and her lovers to go on a road trip with me. I'd gotten out of IHOP. I wasn't a virgin anymore. What the fuck was wrong with me? Why couldn't I be happy?

I hadn't brought any razors with me but Irene had been sleeping with a buck knife for protection. I crawled into the tent and pulled it out from under her pillow. My heart started beating fast. I was starting to feel alive again, like when the deer were biting me, but different. I didn't want Irene to catch me cutting myself. She was freaking out about enough already. Where could I cut myself and still hide it from her? We weren't lying around naked having tons of sex, but that wasn't a guarantee she wouldn't see me naked. I looked down at the ring Irene had bought for me and turned it on my finger. Oh Irene. I pulled it off, revealing a thin tan line. With the tip of the buck knife, I cut a twin wedding ring into my finger. The blade was thick compared to a razor and it burned as I cut through the skin and watched the blood bead up in a circle around my finger.

How come pounding on a typewriter and seeing blood are the only things that make me calm? I needed to get back to San Francisco as soon as possible. To be alone, writing. It was obvious I wasn't in love with Irene anymore—otherwise, why didn't I want to have sex? All her outbursts and talk of living simply was making me feel burdened with responsibility. Maybe I could convince Maria to go on a date with me. . . . The thought of that made me feel immediately guilty. How was I going to live without Irene as my lover? I couldn't imagine but I knew I had to try. I slid my ring back on my finger and felt the sting of the metal rubbing my new cut.

"In my heart, I'll always be married to you, Irene," I whispered.

* * *

When Irene came back from her hike I was napping in the tent. She crawled on top of me and kissed me.

"Hi," I said, moving my mouth away from hers. I tried to look at her, but the dread of trying to break up with her made me turn over.

"What's wrong now?" she said impatiently. "Goaty, if you're this depressed you should think about going on medication."

She had the tone of voice she used to use with Gustavo when she was trying to help him write a paper. My eyes started to well up and I turned back to face her. I looked at her beautiful skull and cheekbones. I could sculpt that face. My stomach bunched in fear but I knew I needed to do this in order to be free.

"I don't know how to tell you this," I started, reaching up to pet her stubbled head. I saw blood trickling out from under the ring.

"I can't be with you. I need to be free."

She looked confused and then that confusion turned to rage.

"I think I'm in love with Maria," I floundered. I wasn't sure that was true, but it felt like it.

"I just quit my job to be with you and you're telling me you want to break up because you think you're in love with your AA sponsor," she yelled.

I tried to pet her head again but she ducked away like the deer had.

"Sshhhh, shhh, it's okay. We can go somewhere. We can talk about this."

"We did go somewhere. We went to Utah to see your friend. We went to the deer petting zoo. We did everything you wanted and now ten days later we're in Arizona and you're ready to go home."

I didn't know what to say. I wanted her to know it wasn't easy for me.

"If you don't think I'm upset you're wrong. I'm upset, about this, too."

"You're upset?! You're upset?!" she cried.

"I just feel really confused. I need time to think. I need to go back to San Francisco."

"Well, let's go if we're going to go," she cried, hurling the pillow into the side of the tent. "Pack up the tent. Pack up this shit."

Everything I thought to say to console her was a lie, so I settled on, "It's not like I'm leaving you entirely. We'll always be friends. And now you can go work with Michael and live communally without worrying about me."

I managed to coax Irene's sobbing self out of the tent so I could break it down and pack everything into the truck. Irene was sobbing and rocking back and forth on the picnic bench just like Camille Claudel when Rodin sent for her to be taken to the mental hospital. We were over. And I'd become the unreasonable father, who for no reason in the middle of a board game starts clapping his giant hands together and says, "Playtime's over kids, let's pack it up."

* * *

I drove us to the nearest motel and checked us in. I was afraid Irene was going to throw a tantrum in the lobby but she just stood catatonically beside me as I paid. Upstairs I ordered a pizza to be delivered and I was so thrilled at the prospect of not eating another Grey Poupon and vegetable sandwich. Irene curled up on the bed, with her arms around herself.

"This doesn't have to be forever," I said, sitting beside her. "We'll figure this all out in the morning after we've both had a good night's sleep."

She seemed to interpret this as some kind of hope. Like after food and a shower, I'd come to my senses.

"I just love you so much," she cried into my chest.

Irene quickly fell into a fitful sleep. I nibbled on the pizza and then tossed and turned, sick from the pain I was causing her. Immediately after I fell asleep I had a waitress stress dream—customers ordered meals off the menu in riddle form that I had to crack. "We'll have the Charlie Chaplin," they said, even though there was no such thing on the menu. I was working at the Tumbleweed Café but everyone still had to wear the IHOP dress. I couldn't understand it and kept complaining to my coworkers. Out of the corner of my eye I saw Irene sitting at a table correcting papers and drinking decaf.

She was on the verge of hysteria, sobbing, "I just want decaf and everyone keeps bringing me regular."

I tried to console her without making it seem like she was my girlfriend because Hope from *Days of Our Lives* was waiting in a car outside for me. I felt self-conscious about Hope seeing me in the IHOP dress and thinking I wasn't tough, so I kept doing stupid things like kicking out windows of nearby parked cars.

Hope was madly in love with me in the dream, and more beautiful than ever. She was literally begging me to kiss her, but I was afraid Irene would catch us. I was telling Hope, "We just broke up. She's still really possessive," but Hope just pulled me toward her and kissed me. It was amazing how effortlessly her soft lips moved against mine. Her mouth tasted like lemons. I couldn't stop nibbling on her ear and giggling, "You taste like lemons," and she kept saying, "I can't believe I'm finally kissing Goaty."

I suddenly remembered Bo.

"What about Bo?" I asked Hope in a panic.

"It's over with him, it's over," she said.

45

BY THE TIME Irene woke up in the morning, I had everything packed in the truck except the few things she'd brought into the motel room. More than ever I knew that I had to get back to San Francisco.

She looked around the packed-up room and said, "What's going on? I thought we were going to talk."

"I love you so much," I said, "but I really need to get back to San Francisco as soon as possible."

I was expecting more tears, but she just got dressed quietly and gave me the silent treatment. When we got to the truck she climbed into the back and got into the fetal position on the sleeping bag.

Even though I hadn't slept, I'd drive straight through to San Francisco. When I got back I'd try to get a job at the Tumbleweed Café. I could start saving again and maybe buy a motorcycle. If I dropped Maria as my sponsor it would be okay to ask her on a date. Changing into the kind of butch girl Maria dated felt daunting, but maybe in time I'd get it right.

* * *

I've been back for a week now in San Francisco. I asked Irene if she could crash with some friends from her old choir group for a few days, so I could try to get my shit together. She's still giving me the silent treatment. William invited Lindsay, the homeless cook from IHOP, to move in with him into my apartment while I was gone and she brought her crazy Doberman, too.

"I thought you were gonna be gone for six months," William said when I unlocked the door of my apartment.

"So did I," I said, setting down my bags.

"Well, at least my clutch is fixed," he joked.

"Do you think it's too late to get your old apartment back?" I asked.

* * *

Irene decided to move into my apartment building because she says this way we'll be in each other's lives every day, even if we're not lovers. Isn't that crazy? For a split second after we got back she considered joining the wind-chime cult, but she said even if we aren't lovers right now she wants to be near me because I'm her only family. And you want to know what's crazier? She's moving into Jenny's old apartment. When I called Maria and told her, she thought I was joking.

"Fucking lesbians," she said, when I swore to her it was the truth.

Everyone in AA keeps asking me if I feel crowded by Irene. I'm just trying to do whatever I can so she doesn't have a nervous breakdown that I left her and she doesn't have a job. It's true I feel nervous about dating other people because she's right down the hall. I don't want to bring someone over and then have Irene knock on my door and start sobbing and throwing things when she sees someone in my apartment.

Even though I want to be Irene's family, too, I feel like I need some space right now. I feel guilty when she calls with her hurt voice, but I'm trying really hard to stay strong. I can't even imagine being

her girlfriend now. Isn't that weird? A month ago I was packing for
our trip. How can feelings change that quickly? Every time I pick up
the phone and she starts crying about us, I feel annoyed. Do you
think I'm a sociopath? She still wants to hang out five times a day
and talk on the phone like before. I just want to work on my book
and not take care of anyone but myself.

* * *

Guess what? I got hired at the Tumbleweed Café. I was so excited I
called Irene to celebrate. We went and got ice cream in the Castro.
Afterward she wanted to buy bongo drums, so I was wandered
around the store while waiting for her.

"Can I help you?" a clerk asked.

"How much is the cello in the window?" I said.

I'd noticed it when I walked in but until I was asked if I needed
help it hadn't occurred to me that I'd actually buy it.

"The cello in the window," he repeated.

"Yeah, how much is it."

He reached into the display and turned the white tag that hung
off a delicate white string. Not a sticker. Not a price code. I was glad
to see someone was still using these old-fashioned white tags. If
Hope from *Days of Our Lives* ever went shopping with me, I would
want only to buy her things that had these simple white tags on
them. She'd understand. She'd been looking for someone her whole
life who'd wanted them as well. I'd found Hope. Not where I was
expecting. But that's the kind of encouragement I needed from life.
I needed to know that if I turned my head to the left, there'd be an
old cello for sale that I could afford in a music store with half-peeled
gold letters on the window. I decided on the spot to become a
famous cellist. I'll even stop writing for a while if it means devoting
myself to being a musician. I won't quit like I quit the harmonica.
This will be different.

"Are you going to buy it?" Irene said.

"Yeah."

"How much are they asking?"

The owner turned the white tag. Someone had written very neatly in black ink, $350. With the almost three thousand dollars left over from the road trip, I could easily afford it.

"I'll buy it," I said to the man, "and I'll need a book that tells me how to play it, too."

I carried it out of the store in its big case. Irene made jokes about my future as a famous cellist, but they were nice jokes. Everything had lightened up. She laughed as I struggled to carry the cello home. It's not heavy, just a little awkward. I liked that people on the street stared at me and wondered if I was a famous musician or not.

* * *

I called my mom this morning and told her I was back in San Francisco. She asked what happened to our six-month plan. I wasn't going to get into it with her but I found myself defending Irene all over again. I think she was trying to get me to say Irene was a bad person, but I refused. When I told her I'd already gotten a new job that seemed to make her feel a little better. I wished there was some way I could only tell her things that wouldn't make her worry.

Then I called Maria and told her how I was going to become a famous cellist and woo the ladies.

"Remember when you weren't even sure you were gay?" she laughed.

I smiled. Something felt different inside me. Like there was a giant heavy scab peeling off and falling away. I didn't care if people thought I was crazy for only making it ten days on a six-month trip. It felt good to be back. And when I wasn't walking on eggshells around Irene, it felt right to be back.

I picked up my cello and tried the first song in the song book, "Twinkle, Twinkle, Little Star." My fingers felt weak trying to hold the strings down, while I pulled the bow across. After a few tries I decided to call my mom back.

"I forgot to tell you I bought a cello," I said.

"Aren't cellos expensive?"

"I had money left over from my trip. Hang on a second." I set the phone on the floor in the front of the cello and concentrated really hard. *Twinkle, twinkle, little star* . . . When I finished and picked up the phone, my mom was clapping.

"I'm going to call you every day and get the cello update," she said excitedly.

There was a lightness in her voice I hadn't heard in a long time.

I hung up the phone, packed up my cello, and got on MUNI. I wanted so badly to be in public with my cello so some woman could see me and ask me out.

One day I'll be a famous cellist, sitting on a stage somewhere, surrounded by beautiful violinists in dresses with thin straps falling off their shoulders, and the light will illuminate their fragile collarbones and the hollows of their necks. We'll play so brilliantly that everyone will burst into a standing ovation and I'll look down, feeling secretly happy but not smiling. I'll finally know what it's like to be surrounded by applause. Afterward a woman who'd been in the audience will come to the reception and find me in a corner. She'll be drinking dark red wine from a goblet while I stare nervously at my feet. We won't need to speak—we won't have to. She'll trace her finger across the big scar on my neck and we'll make out. For the first time in my life I'll feel whole.

I am typing so hard right now. I changed the impression so the keys can really pound away. The whole apartment is filled with sound of the keys clicking and clacking. I wonder if the people downstairs call me the poet.

Ali Liebegott's work has appeared in numerous journals and anthologies. Her first book *The Beautifully Worthless* won the Lambda Literary Award for Debut Fiction. She has performed her work throughout the country, including twice with Sister Spit's Ramblin' Road Show. Liebegott is a recipient of a Poetry Fellowship from the New York Foundation for the Arts. She teaches creative writing at UC San Diego.

MAY 2 9 2012

Made in the USA
Lexington, KY
19 April 2012